Reviews for

He's After Me

Winner of the KYBA and Lancashire Book Award

'Touching, exciting, romantic and convincing in every way.' *Adele Geras Lancashire Book of the Year award judge*

'This is another great novel by Chris Higgins . . . The story moves at a fast pace and is full of drama that always keeps you turning the pages.' *Chicklish*

'A novel affording considerable insight into the maelstrom of adolescent infatuation and its accompanying traumas.' *School Librarian*

'Captured my interest from the beginning and got better and better as I read.' *The Book Bag*

'I just cannot say enough good things about this book. You will be seriously missing out if you don't read it.' *Totally Neevie blog*

'I thank Chris for giving this book an ending that it deserves – just as raw and intense as the rest of the book.' *Loving Books blog*

Hodder
Children's
Books

A division of
Hachette Children's Books

Chris Higgins

shortlisted
Queen
of teen

He's
after
me

Typeset in Berkeley Book by Avon DataSet Ltd,
Bidford on Avon, Warwickshire

Printed and bound in Great Britain by
Clays Ltd, St Ives plc

The paper and board used in this paperback by Hodder Children's Books
are natural recyclable products made from wood grown in
sustainable forests. The manufacturing processes conform to the
environmental regulations of the country of origin.

Hodder Children's Books
a division of Hachette Children's Books
338 Euston Road, London NW1 3BH
An Hachette UK company
www.hachette.co.uk

For my lovely daughters and amazing husband.
Thank you for all your help.

Thanks too to Anne, Naomi and Lindsey.

When they got off the bus it was dark and had started raining. Thrusting his hands deep into his jeans pockets, he watched the girls as they linked arms and dashed straight across the road to the towering warehouse. Quickly he pulled out his camera and snapped them.

They reached the shelter of the lighted entrance and their laughter rang out into the night as they shook their hair free of rain. He snapped them again. Recently converted into apartments, the building was already covered in graffiti.

As the bus pulled away, the blonde one turned to watch and spotted him in the gloom of the bus shelter.

'Who's that?' he heard her say.

The dark one peered at him and he took a step back into the shadows, pulling his hood down low over his face.

'Just some pervert,' she said and leant hard on the buzzer.

'Come on. Dad's waiting.'

Chapter 1

Upstairs, my father opens the door to us, beaming from ear to ear, a large glass of wine in his hand.

'Welcome! Welcome!' he says, his arms wide, sweeping us in like it's a party. 'What a night! What can I get you?'

'What are we celebrating?'

'The weekend? Spending it together? You both making it here at last?'

I ignore the last comment and cast a critical eye around. It's the first time I've been here. The apartment, basically the top floor of a Docklands warehouse, is bright and overheated after the murky dampness outside. Open-plan, with high brick walls and solid oak floors, the windows stretched from floor to ceiling. It must have cost a bomb.

So this is where Dad lives. With Jude, his new girlfriend. Or The Bitch, as Livi prefers to call her. Dad broke Mum's heart when he left her for a younger woman. Much younger. At twenty-six Jude was only nine years older than me.

The Bitch is away for the weekend, which is the reason we are here. Livi's been dying to come for ages, only she won't if Jude is around. She misses Dad dreadfully.

I didn't want to come, only I couldn't think of a good enough reason not to. After all, I've got nothing better to do, now that I've dumped Ben.

'I thought we might order in pizza,' he says. 'Unless you'd rather go out for dinner?'

'Whatever.' I sound about twelve so I add quickly, 'Pizza's fine. It's pissing down outside.'

I sit down on the expensive leather sofa, automatically turning a photograph of Jude, perched proudly on the coffee table beside me, down on its smug, smiling face. Livi ignores him. She's busy scrolling through her text messages with one hand and with the other flicking through the channels on the gigantic TV screen that takes up nearly the whole of one wall.

'Good.' My father pulls his tie off in relief and pours himself another glass of red.

'Can I have one?' asks Livi, without looking up. Dad stares at her uncertainly.

'She's joking,' I say.

4

'No, I'm not.'

He looks embarrassed, caught out, like for a moment he's forgotten just how old Livi actually is. I'm not surprised – she looks way older than fourteen. She could pass for my age easily.

My sister is impulsive, an exhibitionist. A dizzy blonde, true to type. She makes out she doesn't give a stuff about anything but it's mostly an act. Actually, I care less about what people think than she does, though I'm pretty quiet on the whole.

Still waters run deep, says Mum.

Yeah, right. No one's ever waded round in mine long enough to find out. I wish I had more luck with men. I seem to attract them all right. I'm just not that good at keeping them.

Like that boy on the bus. I mean, it was Livi who caught his eye in the first place, singing out loud, but I know for a fact it was me he fancied.

Not everyone was impressed when Livi started singing. She got some black looks which made her sing even louder, and that's when he turned around and grinned at us.

Well, Livi loves an audience, so when we got up to get off at our stop, she practically danced her way down the aisle, just to attract his attention. It worked. As we passed, he looked up and I rolled my eyes at him and he laughed out loud.

But then his smile faded and our eyes held and that's when it happened. A charge passed through me, like an electric shock.

I've never felt anything like it before in my life. It was intense.

I've never been in love.

All the boys I've ever been out with could see that. Some dumped me because I wouldn't put out. Some I dumped because I got bored. Like Ben.

No hard feelings, I said. *Let's stay friends.*

And I meant it. Heart still intact. I never once thought he was The One. Just a nice, kind, safe, unexceptional boy.

But the boy on the bus was different.

'What do you want, Anna?' Dad's studying the pizza menu, his phone in his hand.

'Anything.'

'Olivia?'

Livi's phone bleeps and she scrolls through to read her text. Her face lights up.

'Nothing for me, Dad, I'm going out.'

'What?'

'There's a party on. I won't be late.' She jumps to her feet and grabs her bag.

'*You* are not going anywhere.'

Livi looks at him askance. 'What do you mean?'

'It's pitch dark and pouring with rain. You are not going out in this.'

'I'll get a taxi.'

'I said no. End of.'

Here we go. My little sister's about to kick off because she can't get her own way. I've seen it so many times before and it still does my head in.

'I HATE YOU!' screams Livi. 'YOU'VE RUINED MY LIFE!' She dashes into the bedroom and slams the door as hard as she can. From inside comes the sound of angry sobbing.

'Happy days!' says Dad with a grimace and tops up his glass again before slumping down beside me on the sofa. He pats my knee, like I'm his mate, his ally in all this.

Irritated, I get to my feet and walk over to the huge window with its view over the docks, and lean my head against its cool surface.

It's like a furnace in here. I don't just mean the heating. Livi with her tantrums. Dad with his menopausal affair. Me, overdosing on hormones myself, getting the hots for someone I'll never ever see again.

Outside the rain, sleeting off the sea, drums horizontally

against the glass. Dad's right, it is a filthy night; who would want to be out in this? Down below, small boats clash together in the harbour and the wind whips litter up into the air to disappear over the wall into the gaping black void of the sea.

A movement in the bus shelter across the road catches my eye and I peer down through the driving rain, trying to focus on the one lone person in the world mad enough to be waiting for a bus in this weather.

I breathe in sharply as a current courses through my veins. He is looking up at me.

Feet planted squarely, hands in pockets, chest thrust out, from this angle only his chin is visible beneath his hood. But I know he can see me looking down at him. And I know he is watching me.

Suddenly I am aware how totally exposed I am up here at the very top of the building with all the lights blazing behind me. Anyone could see me out there in the darkness – any nutter or drifter or sad, lonely loser.

I step back so he can't see me any more. My heart is thudding.

When I look back, he's gone.

She'd seen him, he could tell by the way she'd suddenly stepped back from the window. They were up there in the top flat.

Take your time now, he told himself, don't rush things. You've got all the time in the world. You're good at waiting.

Chapter 2

Next morning I wake up on the edge.

Literally.

On the edge of the bed, with Livi's gaping, unconscious mouth exhaling stale morning breath in my face.

From the bedroom next door come Dad's red wine snores. He polished off the first bottle when the pizzas arrived and was well into the second by the time I took myself to bed.

I couldn't sleep. Livi was yakking away on her phone half the night trying to trace the whereabouts of some kid called Ferret who wasn't answering his phone. Ferret! My sister was sending out a missing persons alert for a guy named after a polecat! Now she was dead to the world, exhausted by her failure to track him down.

I can't imagine what it must it be like to care about someone that much.

I shower, dig jeans and various layers out of my bag, and go in search of breakfast. There's not much here hiding in the cupboards, but I help myself to Jude's seriously healthy muesli and splash skimmed milk over it. It's like rabbit food. I can't see my dad eating it.

And then, just to show how little you actually know someone, even if you've lived with them all your life, Dad comes out of his bedroom dressed in running gear. I nearly choke on my dried banana and coconut flakes. He opens the fridge, takes out the orange juice and tosses it straight back from the carton.

'Coming for a jog?' he asks.

I stare at him, rendered speechless by the sight of my father in very short shorts with a discernable paunch, drinking juice from a box.

'Right then,' he says, sounding a bit miffed, 'see you in a bit.' And he's gone.

I watch transfixed through the window as he re-emerges into the square below and does a few stretches. Then he's off, running across the road towards the harbour.

'What you doing?' My sister, bed-haired and panda-eyed, appears at my elbow.

'Look.' We stare down at him together, me still spooning dried fruit and oats into my mouth, Livi in pyjamas, yawning and scratching her armpit, as he makes his way along the side of the harbour, past the boats moored to the wall.

'What is all that about?' I ask wonderingly as he disappears from sight.

'It's The Bitch. It's got to be. She's told him to get rid of his belly.'

'What does she see in him?'

'What does he see in *her*, you mean!' says Livi fiercely and I nod in agreement. But we both know what he sees in her, though we'd never admit it, not even to each other.

Livi sniffs. 'I meant, by the way, what are you doing today?'

'Don't know. Going into town I guess. Meeting Zoe.' The weekend stretches emptily before me. I can't bear the thought of hanging round here with nothing to do. 'I think I might go home after that.'

'Me too. I'm not stopping here if Dad's going to keep me locked up.'

'You're not a prisoner!' I laugh, but then I sober up. 'He's not going to like it, you know, if both of us do a runner. He's made plans for us.'

'Tough. Wait for me, I won't be long.'

But my sister takes ages, as usual, on the phone to her

mates, changing her arrangements each time she talks to someone new. In the end, I get fed up with hanging about so I scrawl a note to Dad to tell him about the change of plan. I feel a bit mean, walking out on him like that.

Then I remember he walked out on us and I slam the door behind me.

At the bus stop I lean back gloomily against the shelter and pull some chewing gum from my pocket. Is this what my life has come to? A weekend with nothing to do and no one to share it with.

'Thanks,' says a voice and I stare in surprise at the hand outstretched before me. It's got a shark tattoo on the wrist. I look up and my heart misses a beat. It's him. The guy on the bus.

'Where's your mate?' he asks. Then he prompts, 'Can I have one?'

'Cheek!' But I drop a piece of gum obediently into his hand. He flicks it up into the air, catches it in his mouth and grins at me.

'Doesn't always work,' he says modestly.

Close up, he's about eighteen or nineteen. Not bad-looking. Pretty fit, actually. His teeth are white against his olive skin and very slightly crooked, which makes him even more attractive. His hair is dark, even darker than mine. I want to touch it.

'Where's your mate?' he repeats. 'The crazy one?'

My mate? The penny drops and so do my hopes. It's Livi he's after, not me.

'Why?' I say. 'You interested?'

'Might be.' He smiles at me lazily, his eyes heavy-lidded. 'But not as interested as I am in you.'

Unbelievably, I feel myself going red but then, thank goodness, the bus arrives and he stands back. 'After you,' he says and I step up on to the platform and fumble around in my bag for my bus pass and I can't find it.

The driver is grumpy, impatient, tutting at my slowness, and my face gets hotter and hotter. I root through the contents of my bag, trying not to show my pyjamas to the world.

At last he waves me on and I make my way to a seat, my cheeks burning, hoping and dreading at the same time that the boy will come and sit beside me.

But when I sit down, he's still standing half on, half off the platform, like he's waiting for someone.

'On or off?' says the bus driver, grumpy old git that he is. 'Make your mind up. I haven't got all day.'

'There's someone running for the bus . . .' he says, and steps back down on to the pavement. But his voice is cut off as the driver closes the doors on him. Through the window I can see my sister running, full-pelt, towards us. Towards him.

As the bus pulls away, Livi comes to a stumbling halt and he throws out his arms to save her.

The last thing I see, as I slump down in my seat, is the pair of them in each other's arms, making identical, one-fingered gestures of derision at the driver and laughing hysterically.

I curse out loud and the woman in front of me turns round and gives me a look of disgust.

At the shopping centre I meet up with Zoe, my best mate, and we go for a coffee. She's recently been dumped by Max, a guy from our A-level Sociology class, and she's finding it really hard. We were double-dating, Zoe and Max, Ben and me. When I packed Ben in, pretty soon after, Max followed suit. I feel a bit guilty about it, actually.

She's going on and on about him, as usual.

'You've got to move on, Zo,' I butt in when I get a chance. 'Get over it!'

'I can't!' she wails. 'I've tried, but it's no good. It's over a month now since we split up and I *still* love him.'

She was in much deeper than me. I sigh deeply, trying to show a bit of understanding. 'It's six months since my mum and dad split up and she's still wrecked.'

'Really?' Zoe stares at me in horror. 'How does she cope?'

'With difficulty.'

The truth is, my mother doesn't. OK, she functions on an everyday level, but that's all she is doing, *functioning*. Since Dad left her for Jude, all the life's seeped out of her. It's like every day she fades away a bit more like an old photograph. I'm afraid one day she'll disappear altogether.

I will *never* let a guy do that to me.

'I read in a magazine once that breaking up is a form of bereavement,' says Zoe gloomily.

'Really?'

'Yeah, only it's worse in a way. Especially if the corpse is still around, chatting someone else up before your eyes.'

We go shopping to cheer ourselves up, trawling in and out of stores. Zoe spends a small fortune on random stuff, but my heart's not in it. I don't know what's the matter with me today.

'Isn't that your sister?' says Zoe. I follow her eyes and spot Livi, easily identifiable by her cropped, blonde hair and her loud laugh. She's in the middle of a noisy gang of kids. I recognize a couple of them from when I was at school. Troublemakers. At least she's not still with Bus Boy.

Zoe shakes her head in disbelief. 'What is she doing with *them*?'

People are attracted to Livi like bees to a bright, beautiful flower. She stands head and shoulders above the rest of us boring bedding plants. But the trouble is, she attracts wasps too. There's one buzzing round her now, hands everywhere, touching her every chance he gets . . .

Get your hands off my little sister! I scream inside.

'Anna!' Livi sees me and immediately detaches herself from his clutches, bounding over to greet me. I know what she's doing, she doesn't want me to see who she's hanging out with, but it's too late. The boy follows behind, hovering over her like a hornet.

'Who's this? Aren't you going to introduce me?'

Livi looks nervous.

'This is Steven. Ferret, this is my sister, Anna.'

So this is the celebrated Ferret. I study him. He's not that tall, about the same height as her, with fair hair sticking out from beneath a black beanie. He's quite good-looking but his face is a bit too thin, his nose too long, and his eyes too small for my taste.

'Ferret,' I say. 'Suits you.'

The eyes harden. 'What's that supposed to mean?'

'Nothing. It's your name, not mine.'

Livi laughs nervously. 'His name's Steven Ferris. That's why he's called Ferret.'

Great. I've insulted him without even meaning to. He stares me out, pale eyes narrowed. When I drop my gaze he gives a victorious, insolent little bark of a laugh, like he's won, and turns away.

I'm furious.

'What are you doing with *that*?' I hiss.

Livi's face falls. 'Loads of girls like him. He's dead fit.'

'No he's not, Liv. You can do so much better than him!'

She shakes her head. 'You don't know him!'

'I don't want to know him!'

'Get lost!' she says and now *she* turns away.

'Livi! Don't be daft!'

'Piss off!' she yells at me.

Behind her, her mates burst out into shrieks of laughter.

All except Ferret, who stands there staring silently at me, a twisted, malevolent smile on his pale, pinched face.

I turn on my heel and walk away.

He watched as she disappeared down the mall with her fat friend in tow. He'd got her measure now. One of those girls who thinks she knows everything. Thinks she's better than everyone else.

Well, you can be too clever for your own good.

He could teach her a thing or two. He could show her.

Chapter 3

'What the hell does she see in him?' gasps Zoe as we walk off.

'Goodness knows!'

'He gives me the creeps.'

'Me too!' I don't want to admit it, but I'm feeling a bit freaked out after that encounter, like I've been threatened or something. 'Actually, Zoe, I think I'm going to make a move now, if it's OK with you.'

'See you Monday.' Zoe gives me a hug. I make my way through the mall, head down, trying to avoid the couples with their arms wrapped around each other. Am I the only single in the world? Suddenly I go slap-bang into someone. I hear them grunt like the air's been knocked clean out of them and my bag goes flying.

'Sorry!' I say. 'My fault. Sorry!'

'You!'

I stare into a pair of surprised eyes. I don't believe it! It's him again. The boy from the bus. I look around for my bag but he beats me to it. He picks it up along with its scattered contents and hands it back to me. Our hands touch. I can feel my cheeks burning.

'Are you stalking me?' he says.

'No!'

'Only we keep bumping into each other.'

'I never saw you before last night!'

'And this morning.' He grins and I realize he's winding me up. He's gorgeous when he smiles. 'Do you live in the Docklands?'

'No. My dad does. With his girlfriend.'

'That old warehouse they've done up?'

'Yeah, Wharfside. Top floor.'

He nods, studying me, like he likes what he sees. 'What's she like?'

'Who?'

'The girlfriend?'

He obviously wants to talk. I shrug my shoulders and the corner of my mouth curls. He laughs out loud. 'That good, hey?'

'We call her The Bitch.'

'Some girls are,' he says and nods understandingly. I wonder if he's been hurt. His dark eyes are studying me. 'Look,' he says, then he hesitates, like he's about to say something important and doesn't know how. My heart starts racing. He's going to ask me out.

'Anna? Anna!'

Oh no! I'd know that voice anywhere. I turn around to see my father waving at me. Behind him, Jude emerges from a shop doorway. I groan aloud.

'That's all I need. My dad – and he's got The Bitch with him.'

The boy's eyes shift past me and he takes a step backwards.

'See you around then,' he says and I want to say, 'No, wait!' but instead I echo, 'Yeah, see you around,' and he walks away.

Thanks, Dad. You don't just screw your own relationships up, you screw mine too.

The only guy I've been remotely interested in for ages and I don't even know his name.

Chapter 4

By Saturday night I'm totally pissed off.

I didn't waste much time talking to Dad and Jude, needless to say. It was pretty obvious by the speed in which The Bitch had appeared back on the scene that her weekend away was a fabrication. Once she'd discovered the fledglings had flown the nest, the cuckoo was straight back in.

Mum's out when I get home and there's no sign of Livi, surprise, surprise. I bung a pizza in the oven, forgetting until I sit down to eat it that I'd had one last night. There's nothing worth watching on television so I put on a DVD, but I've seen it before too many times.

I go on Facebook. Mistake. I trawl through pics of people off their heads and reply to messages from people having the best time of their lives.

Why is everyone else having a better life than me? I ask

myself. And how come I have so many hundreds of friends online, but no one to spend Saturday night with?

Not quite true. Ben has asked me if I want to try again. He does this all the time. Tonight I'm almost tempted because I'm so fed up. But you can't *try* to love someone. You either do or you don't. And liking's not enough.

Heaving a big, sad sigh, I go to switch the computer off. Then I pause. I have a new friend request.

It's from Jem Smith.

Who's Jem Smith?

Who cares? I need all the friends I can get.

Confirm.

His profile comes up. I click on the picture to make it bigger and my heart soars.

It's him!

How did he know my name?

A new message has appeared.

The lounge door opens. It's Mum. Both of us jump a mile.

'Don't do that!'

'What?'

'Sneak up on me like that!'

'I thought you were at your father's for the weekend. Where's Livi?'

'With her mates.'

She looks contrite. 'I'm sorry, darling, I wouldn't have gone out if I'd known you were here on your own.'

'Mum, I'm fine.'

She comes and stands beside me.

God, she wants to talk.

'Decided not to stay at the apartment then?'

'No.'

Silence as she waits for more. She wants to know what it's like there and why I decided to come home, but she doesn't want to pry. After a while, she says, 'Are you on Facebook?'

'Yes.'

She looks at the screen. I minimize it.

'Who are you talking to?'

'A friend.'

She gives up with a sigh. 'Right then, I'm off to bed. Don't stay up all night.'

'I won't.'

As soon as she's out of the door, I open the screen and click on the message. It says:

Enjoy your chocolate fix!

What chocolate fix?

Suddenly I jump to my feet and grab my bag, pulling out the contents. Phone, wallet, door keys, make-up, hairbrush, tissues, chewing gum, couple of receipts.

And a champagne chocolate heart.

I log on to Facebook Chat and he's logged in too. I start writing to him straight away.

> *Thanks. How did that get into my bag?*
> *It's a secret.*
> *How did you know how to reach me?*
> *That's a secret too.*
> *You shouldn't have.*
> *Why not?*
> *You don't know me.*
> *I could get to know you.*
> *Yes you could.*
> *Want to meet up next week?*
> *Yes.*
> *I'll be in touch.*

I close down the computer and stare at the chocolate heart. It's a tacky and overpriced cliché. But, apart from the occasional Valentine card over the years, it's the first time anyone has ever declared their interest in me through a symbol.

My head sees the shiny paper disguising the inferior chocolate.

My heart sees a mysterious, dark-haired boy who's

worked out a way of getting in touch with me.

That is so romantic.

He felt restless now, bored. Time to get out for a while. He needed his fix.

He was almost out of the door before he remembered to change into dark clothes. You don't want to be seen, he reminded himself. Stay out of sight, be invisible.

It was amazing what you could get up to when no one knew you were there.

Chapter 5

All week I'm waiting for Jem to get in touch with me but he doesn't. I can't concentrate on a thing. I check Facebook every five minutes but he's not on it. As the days go by, I drag Zoe along to the mall after college but there's no sign of him. I even consider getting the bus over to the Docklands in case that's where he hangs out, but I manage to stop myself.

'Message him,' says Zoe, but I won't. I've got more pride than that.

'He knows where to find me.'

'Maybe he's one of those guys for whom the thrill of the chase is everything,' says Zoe thoughtfully. 'Now you've agreed to go out with him, he's no longer interested.'

'Since when were you such an authority on men?' I say grimly and she shuts up.

Then she adds with a grin, 'I don't believe he exists. You made him up, sad creature. He's a figment of your lonely imagination,' and she makes me laugh.

But inside, I'm gutted. He was different from anyone I'd ever met. Now he's disappeared off the scene I realize how much I liked him. And I thought that he liked me.

As time goes on and there's no sign of Jem, I start to think Zoe was right about him after all. Not about existing – he was real, all right. But he must've been just trying it on.

I come to the conclusion once and for all that you can't trust men, and try not to let it get me down. I've got A levels to get on with and, soon, uni to apply for. Who needs them anyway?

Gradually I settle back to college work. I've had my eyes focused on Newcastle for ages. Great course and loved the city when I went up to have a look round. The competition's fierce though, I can't afford to slack. Not that I would.

All I want now is to get away from this place. Go to uni and have a good time.

And then, all of a sudden, he's back.

Chapter 6

He turns up out of the blue one day, just when I'd given up on him completely. His timing is impeccable.

He's waiting for me outside college, leaning against the wall opposite the front gates. It's Zoe who spots him first. She nudges me in the ribs.

'Nice!' she says. 'Take a look at that.'

'Who?'

'That boy over there. He's staring at us.'

I follow her direction and my heart misses a beat. It's him! Our eyes meet and he unfolds himself and stands up straight, his face breaking into a smile. He's taller than I remember.

'Wow!' breathes Zoe. 'D'you know him?'

'It's him,' I say simply. 'It's Jem.'

'Hi,' he says, coming over. 'I've been away. I'm sorry. But I'm back now.'

I wonder where he's been. Far enough away not to be on Facebook. Is there anywhere that far?

But his 'Sorry' sounds genuine. And I like 'I'm back now.' Like he's back in the place where he's meant to be.

'How did you know where to find me?'

'Oh, I've got ways and means.'

'Such as?'

He taps the side of his nose and grins, like he's saying: *Keep this out of it*. I shake my head, trying not to smile.

What is it with him? He's so secretive, so elusive. I've never met anyone quite like him before. I hold his gaze, determined to appear unimpressed, and he laughs softly, like he can read my mind.

'Drink?' he asks.

'What, now?' I dart a quick look at Zoe, standing behind me, taking it all in. We were going to hers.

'It's OK,' she says quickly. 'I'll see you tomorrow.'

I wonder if he's going to insist she comes with us, but he gives her his lazy smile and says, 'See you,' and she walks away. And then it's just him and me.

One minute we're heading up the road together and I'm trying desperately to think of something to say and the next minute, to my surprise, he's leapt on to the platform of a bus waiting at a crossroads.

'Come on!' he yells, reaching out his hand for me. 'The lights are changing!'

I run after the bus as it lurches away and grab his hand. He pulls me on and I stumble into his arms.

'Thanks,' I say, looking up into his face. His arms tighten as he laughs down at me. His eyes are crinkled, and when he smiles one side of his mouth lifts slightly higher than the other.

I want to kiss it.

He lets me go and bounds upstairs to the top deck. When I follow him up, he's already sprawled at the front of the bus, feet up on the windscreen, arm along the back of the seat. I sit down beside him.

'Mind telling me where we're going?'

His hand moves to rest lightly on my shoulder. It feels good, like I belong to him.

'Wherever you want, Anna,' he says.

We end up down at the harbour, not that far from my dad's place. We climb up on to the harbour wall to watch the waves crashing against the rocks. Before long we're soaked but I don't care. I feel wild and free, like the sea beneath me.

Jem runs along the wall, arms spread wide, as sure-footed and agile as a panther. I tell him to be careful and so he stands on his toes, right at the edge, his back to the

39

sea, deliberately taunting me. He starts swaying like mad as if he's lost his balance, his arms making huge circles. I can't help it, I close my eyes – and that's when he yells. I scream out loud, convinced he's fallen over the wall into the churning sea. But when I open my eyes he's still there, laughing at me.

I punch him and he puts his arms round me.

And then he kisses me.

Later, soaked through to the skin and shaking with cold, we take refuge under the awning of a boat, away from prying eyes. Jem wraps me in his arms but I can't get warm.

'You got me here under false pretences!' I protest, my teeth chattering. 'You said you were taking me for a drink!'

'I am,' he says and peers through the window of the boat. Then, quick as a flash, before I can say anything, he slips off his jacket, wraps it around his fist and punches out the glass. Putting his hand inside, he fiddles around for a bit, his face rapt, then the door swings open. 'We're in,' he says, pushing me inside. 'After you.'

'Jem!' I splutter, but he laughs at my shocked face.

'Go on,' he says. 'It's OK. It belongs to a friend of mine.'

'He's not going to be very happy when he sees

what you've done to his window,' I remark. 'Where's the light?'

'Leave it,' he orders. I peer round the dark interior. I can just about make out built-in wrap-around seating, a table and lots of little cupboards. Jem starts opening them. He chucks me some towels out of one and exclaims with delight when he finds a small fridge in another. 'Trust a sailor to have booze on board,' he declares triumphantly, holding up some cans of beer. 'Make yourself at home.'

I sit on the floor and sip my beer while Jem towels my hair dry. Then I do the same for him. I've never done that for anyone before, except Livi. But this is different.

Afterwards we sit huddled together in a blanket for warmth, watching the moon rising over the bay. The boat rocks us gently. With my head on Jem's shoulder, I listen to the sound of the sea lapping beneath us and I don't think I've ever been so happy. We talk and we talk and we talk and then we kiss.

And that's how it all begins.

And so love's arrow finds its target.

And she'd seemed such a sensible girl too, not the kind to lose her head over some bloke.

That's love for you.

Chapter 7

Although I longed to fall in love, I always thought it was such a crazy, dangerous thing to do. A huge leap of faith. Like tombstoning. Maybe that's the attraction. When you jump into it, you have no idea what lies beneath the surface. And once you've made that leap into the unknown, there's no going back. It's risky and scary and could so easily end in disaster.

But with Jem, it's easy. I try to explain it to Zoe.

'It's like I've drifted off to sleep on a hot beach and found myself in some parallel-dream-world that I never knew existed.'

'Cheesy!' she says.

I know what I sound like. Sentimental. Smug. But I can't help it. 'Honestly, Zo, Jem is the perfect boyfriend. He's good-looking, he's romantic, he's thoughtful . . .'

'You hardly know him!'

'Of course I know him. He's so reliable, you wouldn't believe. He even texts me if he's going to be a few minutes late.'

'He's always texting you!' My phone bleeps obligingly and she rolls her eyes.

It's him. I read the message and smile to myself.

'What does he say?'

'He's missing me.'

Zoe groans. 'I can't stand much more of this. It's not fair. Has he got any mates?'

I shake my head. 'Not that I know of.'

'Come on, Anna, introduce me!'

'He hasn't,' I say. It's the truth. We've been going out together for weeks now and he's never once introduced me to a friend. 'He's a bit of a loner. He seems to be happy just spending time with me.'

'Lucky you,' sighs Zoe.

'I know I am.' Lucky to have had the sense to choose someone who wants to be with me as much as I want to be with him. And who would never ever let me down. Not like poor Livi.

'Ferret stood Livi up again last night,' I say. 'He's a complete jerk.'

Zoe snorts. 'I could've told her that in the first place.'

'I *did* tell her that in the first place, but she wouldn't

listen. She's finding it out for herself now though.'

Poor Livi is besotted with Ferret. She is completely at his beck and call and spends her life moping about for the next text, the next change of plan. It's obvious to everyone but her that the little shit is backing off. I'm worried sick it's because he's got what he wanted. But I can't ask her.

Maybe it's not just luck that I chose the good guy. Maybe it's judgement. Let's face it, even when I was fourteen, I would never have fallen for Feral Boy. I've got too much pride.

Though, if I'm totally honest, I think it was Jem who chose me, not the other way round.

'What's he up to at the moment?' asks Zoe. 'Apart from ringing you up a couple of hundred times a day?'

'Working on his portfolio,' I start to explain but, right on cue, my phone rings again and Zoe rolls her eyes.

'I can't see you tonight,' he says and my heart plummets. 'I've got to work.'

'OK.'

'It's not OK. It's rubbish,' he says and I can imagine his face, dark and scowling. 'But it's overtime. They're paying me time and a half. I could do with the money.'

'No problem.'

'Shall I turn it down?' he asks.

'No way! I could do with a night in. I've got bags of

work to do for college.' It's true actually. I'm seeing so much of Jem, my work is beginning to suffer.

And I know how much he needs the money.

Jem is a photography student in London. He's down here for a while doing a project on the regeneration of the Docklands. To make ends meet, he works at the new hotel down there as a kitchen porter. Free accommodation, but he shares a room with two guys with smelly feet and a curry and lager habit.

'I'll make it up to you, I promise. We'll go somewhere nice on my night off.'

'Great. What are you doing now?'

'Looking at photos.'

'Of?' I know the answer already but I want to hear him say it.

'Some beautiful girl.'

Last night Jem was snapping away at me like the paparazzi. That's what happens when your boyfriend is doing a photography degree. Forget about the docks, I'm his favourite subject.

I asked him why he chose the Docklands as a topic and he said it was because years ago he'd lived round here for a short time with his grandmother, while his mother was in prison for fraud.

His background is horrendous. Not that he goes on

about it a lot. But sometimes it drip-feeds into the conversation and yet another terrible truth leaks out from his past.

The amazing thing is, he's emerged from the chaos of his life completely sane. It puts into perspective all those excuses that are made for people's conduct. You know, all the way through school, I heard allowances being made for disruptive behaviour. *'He's a bad lad but what can you expect?' 'Family like his, what chance has he got?'*

Well, I've got news for you, it doesn't have to be like that. No one could have had a more shambolic upbringing than Jem and he's the nicest person I know.

'You're supposed to be taking photos of the docks, not me,' I remind him.

He chuckles. 'You're more interesting. And better-looking.'

Right response. You're so good for my self-esteem, Jem. I'm almost starting to believe it myself.

Chapter 8

On my way home from college that evening I bump into Jude, of all people, clip-clopping along the street in suit and high heels, hair scraped back in work mode, briefcase under her arm. It's her voice I hear first, on the phone – to my dad, presumably.

'Honestly, you would not *believe* the day I've had . . .'

It's so distinctive. She has this habit of emphasizing one particular word in each sentence. When she catches sight of me, her face stretches into a fixed, professional smile. 'Ring you back,' she says and slips her phone into her bag.

'Anna! How *are* you?'

'Fine.'

'How's Livi?'

'Fine.'

'Your mum?'

I don't deign to reply. Jude is used to firing questions at people and getting answers, but fortunately I don't happen to be one of her clients. She's a lawyer who spends her life defending petty criminals and little toe-rags who've broken the terms of their ASBOs.

Most people are in awe of her, my mother included, for having such a high-profile career by the age of twenty-six, but I reckon it sounds more glamorous than it is. It stands to reason she must spend most of her working week mixing with losers and perverts. Shame.

'Your dad was *so* pleased to have you to stay – it's been *ages* . . .' she gushes. 'You and Livi *must* come over again.'

Condescending cow! Who does she think she is? I don't need an invitation to see my own father. 'I'm busy at the moment,' I say, my voice cold as ice, but she nods sympathetically.

'A levels, hey? I remember it well.'

You should do, it wasn't exactly that long ago. Her tone, dripping with solicitude, infuriates me. How dare she assume that the only thing in my life is exams?

'Actually, I'm seeing someone.'

Why did I tell her that? It's none of her business.

I know why. To make myself feel better. To show her I have a life beyond grumpy-stepdaughter-who-came-with-the-guy mode. Jude always lumps Livi and

52

me together and reduces me to Truculent Teenager With Attitude.

'*Are* you? That's *great*! What's his name?'

'Jem.'

'James?' she says, mishearing. 'Is he at college with you?'

'No, he's at uni.'

'A *student*!' she enthuses. 'How lovely. *Where?* What does he study?'

Jude went to Bristol to study Law. 'One of the hardest degrees at one of the top universities in the country,' Dad informed us once. Photography at some obscure London college of higher education doesn't begin to compete with that.

'Oxford. He's reading Medicine.' Where did that come from? Flying out of my mouth before my brain was in gear. If I wanted to impress her, it worked. Jude's eyes open wide in surprise.

'*Really?* You must bring him round for dinner one night, Anna. We'd love to meet him.'

I bet you would! 'Right,' I say unenthusiastically.

'I *mean* it. He sounds so interesting.'

'He is.' Actually, he's far, far more interesting than you think. He has a split personality. Jem is studying Photography in London while working as a kitchen porter down here, while James is studying Medicine at Oxford. At the same time.

I groan inwardly. How the hell did I get myself into this? It's all Jude's fault, with her incessant questions. And now it's too late to take it back.

At this point I make a firm resolution to keep my boyfriend as far away from her as possible.

On her own today, the boyfriend must be working.

It made him sick to think of them, what they must get up to when they were alone together.

Chapter 9

At home, Livi is busy getting ready for a night out. St Wilfred's Big Party Night. Highlight of the social calendar, *if* you're between the ages of eleven and fourteen. Actually, I'm surprised that Livi is so up for it; I thought she was way too cool for school.

But it turns out it's a special charity night, a bit like a prom, with prizes for best-dressed couple, most popular couple, freakiest couple, etc. Needless to say, Ferret is her date for the evening, so I point out to her that they have a good chance of winning the last one, but she thinks I'm joking.

'Best-dressed for us,' she says, 'every time!'

She does look gorgeous in a typically over-the-top way for what is, when all is said and done, a school disco. She's wearing a red dress that clings to her amazing figure but stops just short of looking tarty. I'll say one thing for my kid sister, for her age she has style. She's spent a long time on her hair and make-up, you can tell. Which is why I'm kind of surprised by her choice of footwear.

'You need heels with that outfit,' I say as she wriggles her feet into her pumps.

'Nah, it's OK, I want to dance.'

I stare at her in disbelief. This is Olivia talking, who wore her six-inch heels all through summer until her feet bled and Mum donated them to Oxfam. Then the light dawns. 'Oh, I get it . . .'

She frowns and ignores me, but we both know what I mean. Ferret isn't that tall. In her heels she'd tower over him. He wouldn't like that, would he?

Catch me ever changing my appearance for the sake of some guy's ego.

Mum shakes her head at me imperceptibly to deflect a row. 'What time is Steven coming to pick you up?'

'Um . . .' Livi looks uncertain. 'Not sure. I think I might be meeting him there.' She grabs her phone and dashes off to put a search out on his whereabouts.

'He can't even be arsed to come and get her,' I say in disgust.

Mum sighs. 'Not all men are as nice as Jem. Give him a chance, Anna. He's just a boy.'

'He's a little rat,' I say. And two minutes later, when

Livi rushes off all in a dither because, even though she can't locate him, she doesn't want to keep him waiting, Mum looks as if she might agree with me for once.

I settle down when she's gone and start making inroads into my college work. I'm more behind than I thought. It's piled up over the past few weeks since I've been spending so much time with Jem. I can't blame him, it's my choice, but I need to get back down to it if I want to get into Newcastle.

Out in the hall, the phone rings. I can hear Mum jabbering away, then she sticks her head around the door.

'I'm going over to Karen's. She's a bit upset.'

Karen, who works with Mum, is always upset. She's going through a messy divorce at the moment and she and Mum are 'there' for each other. Which means the pair of them meet up constantly to drown their sorrows over medicinal bottles of dry white wine.

I move on to Sociology. An essay is overdue. I've never been behind with my work before. I put everything else firmly out of my mind and buckle down to it.

Two hours and five pages later, I'm concentrating so hard that I jump when my phone rings. It's got to be Jem.

But I'm wrong.

On the end of the phone, someone is crying. Loud, ugly, racking sobs, like a soul in torment. It's one of the scariest sounds I've ever heard in my life and totally freaks me out.

'Who is this?'

'An-na?' My name is a choked, broken whisper.

Livi!

'Livi, what is it? Answer me. Tell me what's wrong.'

I'll kill him. I'll kill if he's done something to her. I'll strangle him with my bare hands.

'What's happened? Livi, stop crying. Tell me!'

She's been in a fight. I can't believe it. And come off the loser, by the sound of it.

'Where are you?'

'Outside school.'

'Who are you with?'

'No-bo-dy!' The wails start up again.

'Stay where you are. I'm coming to get you, right this minute. Don't move, Livi. I'm on my way.'

I grab my coat and make for the door, wondering if I should leave a note for Mum to say where I've gone. No, too complicated, it will only worry the life out of her.

Outside, the night is wild. Rain sleets down on me as I make my way towards the taxi-rank on the main street. In

ten minutes we draw up outside the school. I have just
enough money in my pocket to pay the taxi-driver. I make
a bee-line for reception, ablaze with lights, but then hear
my name being called from the shadows of the car park.

'Anna?'

'Livi?'

My sister emerges into the light. She's a wreck. Her
hair is a mess, her nose is bleeding and black mascara
tracks run down her face. The classy new dress has been
torn at the shoulder and the hem is hanging down. She's
sobbing, fit to burst.

I fling my arms around her. 'Who did this to you?'

'Cora.'

I remember Cora Pugh when she started at St Wilfred's.
She was a mean, hard-faced cow, even in Year 7.

'I'll slaughter her! Where is she? She's not going to get
away with this. I'll report her. I'll tell the Head. Come with
me . . . !' I grab hold of Livi, furious, but she resists.

'No, Anna. Leave it there.'

'She attacked you, Livi!'

'No. It was me. I started it.'

'What?' I stare at my sister aghast. 'What do you mean?'

'I started it,' she repeats. 'It was all my fault.'

Chapter 10

Poor Livi. She explains it all to me as we make our way home.

There'd been no sign of Ferret when she got to school and he wasn't answering his phone. She hung round for ages waiting, working herself up into a state. After a while, with everyone else in couples, she took herself off to the loo to shed bitter tears.

When she came out he was there, and Cora was snogging him. She was so angry she marched straight over and slapped her. Cora slapped her back. A fight ensued and was broken up by teachers. She started it, so she was thrown out.

'D'you know what the worst thing is?' she says to me between sobs. 'It wasn't her fault. She didn't know I was still going out with him. He'd told her he'd dumped me.'

'That's what she says,' I say grimly. But it's probably

63

true. That's exactly the sort of lie I would expect Ferret to tell. Two-timing little rat.

'Come on. Let's get you home.'

We don't have enough money between us for a taxi, so I slip my arm through my sister's and together we dash across the main road, dodging a stream of orange headlights, to take a short-cut through the multi-storey car park to the bus station.

The car park is bleak and dimly lit at this time of night. It's a horrible concrete jungle of a place, with graffiti sprayed all over the walls. Row upon row of silent cars stand brooding and there are dark, sinister corners where anyone could be lying in wait for you.

But my sister has had enough. She can't take any more, and I need to get her home. So I grit my teeth and march her through it, my senses on high alert, eyes darting this way and that.

Something is scuttling in a corner. Automatically we grip each other tight.

'You're never more than three metres from a rat in Britain,' whispers Livi, looking petrified.

Don't we know it! 'Or a ferret,' I whisper back and am rewarded by a giggle that bubbles up out of nowhere.

We move on as one, glued tight to each other, stiff

with apprehension. From the corner of my eye I think I see something moving, a shadow, a shape . . . I quicken our pace, Livi stumbling along beside me. In front of us a concrete stairway leads up to the next storey . . . Anyone could be up there, lurking . . .

Suddenly, from somewhere above us, comes a dreadful, unearthly wail, like something in torment. I nearly jump out of my skin and Livi screams. We cling to each other as it goes on and on and on . . .

'Car alarm!' I say and we collapse in relief. 'Come on, let's get out of here! I hate this place.'

But the next second there's a skittering, clattering, stamping noise, and down the concrete stairway bounds a guy in jeans and sweats, hood knotted well down over his face. I pull Livi out of his way as he leaps the last set of steps and goes sprawling on the ground, hands outstretched in front of him. My heart misses a beat. In a split second he's up and vaulting the barrier, then he disappears outside into the night.

Within seconds a uniformed security guard appears, puffing and panting, in his bright day-glo jacket.

'Did you see him?' he gasps.

I nod.

'Would you recognize him again?'

Livi shakes her head, scared stiff. 'It was all too fast.'

'You couldn't see his face,' I say truthfully.

The guard swears loudly and turns away, speaking into his radio. I grab Livi's arm.

'Quick!' I say, not wanting to get caught up in all this. 'Let's go.'

On the bus I ring Jem, but his phone is turned off. I curse under my breath.

'I thought you said he was working tonight,' says Livi.

'He is.'

'Well, he's not going to be able to answer his phone, is he?'

'No, I guess not.' I stare out of the window, lost in thought.

After a while she says in a small voice, 'Are you mad at me, Anna?'

'No.'

'Don't tell Mum what happened, will you?'

I turn my head to look at her. 'Clean yourself up a bit then or she's going to notice.'

She takes out a mirror and some wipes and starts to repair the damage. By the time she's run a comb through her hair and reapplied her make-up she's looking more or less back to normal.

'All right?'

'You'll do.'

'Are you sure you're not mad at me?'

'I said no, didn't I?'

'Are you mad at Jem?'

'Now, why would I be mad at Jem?'

'I don't know. But you've gone all moody since you tried to ring him.'

'Don't be daft,' I say. 'You're imagining it.'

But she isn't.

He had to be more careful. He couldn't afford to get caught.

Next time he might not be so lucky.

The last thing he wanted was for them to find out what he was really up to.

Chapter 11

Unbelievably, when we get home at last, Mum is still out. She arrives back half an hour later, by which time Livi is safely tucked up in bed and I'm in front of the computer once more, trying to get back into my Sociology essay. But my heart's not in it.

'Sorry I've been so long,' she says as she lets herself in. 'Poor old Karen, she's in a bit of a tizz. How's the work going?'

'All right,' I say grimly as she comes over to hug me. Her breath stinks of wine. I'm trying not to panic at the thought of how much I've still got to get through.

'Did Livi have a good time?'

'Think so. She's fast asleep. I'm going up too.'

Upstairs, I press Jem's number again for the umpteenth time since I got home, but there's still no reply. Miserably, I get into bed and pull the duvet over me. And eventually fall asleep.

*

I know it's not right. What's it doing here, in the car park?

Sharks live in the ocean. Sharks are not urban predators. They don't lurk in multi-storeys, stalking people on their way home from a night out.

But this shark is special. It's waiting for me.

A ringing noise. Save me, please . . .

*

I wake in the pitch darkness to the sound of my phone and fumble for it blindly. My heart is racing. It was a dream, that's all. A weird dream.

'Anna?'

'Jem? Is that you?'

'Anna. I'm sorry. I've just got your calls. My phone was turned off at work. Is anything wrong?'

He sounds anxious.

'No. Well, yes. I missed you.'

'I missed you too. Are you sure you're all right? You sound upset.'

'I was dreaming. A nightmare. You woke me up.'

'I'm sorry. It was manic tonight. We never stopped. I've only just finished.'

I glance at the clock. It's gone two a.m.

'It was a good little earner though. Means I can afford to take you out somewhere.'

'That's nice. I got some work done.'

'Well done.' He sounds like Jem again, now he knows I'm OK. My heartbeat returns to normal as his familiar voice calms me down. 'I missed you,' he repeats.

'Me too. You'll never guess what happened to Livi . . .'

I launch into a lengthy explanation and he listens carefully, expressing outrage on Livi's behalf and describing in detail what he intends to do to Ferret when he gets hold of him.

'You sound like her big brother!' I say teasingly.

There's silence for a moment, then he says, 'Well, I suppose I am, in a way,' and he sounds really pleased, like I've paid him a compliment. We carry on talking for a while, his voice comforting in the darkness, like a kiss.

'See you tomorrow,' he says at last. 'Sleep well.'

'See you tomorrow,' I echo and click off, though not before I add automatically, 'Love you,' just like I do when I'm saying goodnight to Mum or Livi.

I suck in my breath, rigid with embarrassment as I realize what I've just said.

'Anna,' I groan. 'You and your big mouth!'

My phone bleeps. A text from Jem.

Love you too.

I hug the message to myself in the darkness. It's OK.
He loves me too.

But then my smile fades and I begin to feel really,
really bad.

I doubted him.

I can't believe I did that.

It was just seeing that shark tattoo on that guy's
wrist tonight. The guy in the car park. It freaked me out.
I mean, they're not that common, are they, shark tattoos?
I've never seen one before.

I thought it might be him. I thought my boyfriend was
a car thief.

I turn my face into the pillow and groan. 'Anna, you
are an idiot!'

How could you? After all that Jem's been through. All
he wants is to be with you but instead he works an extra
shift in a grotty hotel kitchen to make some money to take
you out. He would do anything for you, for Livi.

Because he loves you.

And what do you do to repay him? Suspect him of
breaking into cars.

Well, he broke into that boat, didn't he? says the nagging
little voice inside my head.

That was different, it belonged to a mate of his.

Jem hasn't got any mates.

Stop it! Stop it! I hurl my pillow on to the floor and sit up, my head in a whirl. Then I take some slow, deep breaths, until the nagging voice subsides and finally shuts up.

Don't do this! I tell myself firmly. You'll spoil everything with your nasty, suspicious mind.

Jem is the best thing that ever happened to you.

Sugar and spice and all things nice – that's what little girls are made of.

Not all of them are nice though.

He knew that better than anyone.

Look at these two. Good sister/bad sister.

Which one would get what was coming to her?

Chapter 12

Jem and I are becoming closer and closer. We spend as much time together as we can, though it's difficult sometimes with work and college. When I can't see him, he texts me all the time to see what I'm up to. Zoe says it would do her head in to have a bloke on her tail like that all the time.

She's jealous.

At college they tell us the UCAS forms are now ready online. It's time to think about uni.

'Newcastle?' says Mum, knowing it's always been my ultimate goal.

'Hopefully.'

'You are getting your work done, aren't you?' she asks, sounding concerned.

'Of course I am!' I say, and she believes me because I've always got my work done, I've always been conscientious.

But, the truth is, I'm falling behind.

It's Jem's fault. I can't resist him.

Livi thinks he's wonderful too.

One day after school, Ferret comes up and apologizes to her in front of everyone for the way he's behaved. Nobody could believe what they were hearing, he's such an arrogant little shit normally. It made Livi's day. She came home beaming, her self-esteem restored.

It had to be Jem's doing. She said she could swear she saw him outside her school talking to her ex just before Ferret came over and apologized. By the time she'd picked herself up off the floor with shock, Jem had disappeared.

He wouldn't admit it though when he came round that night. He just grinned and said, 'Nobody messes with my little sister,' in a croaky Italian accent like that guy from *The Godfather*. From that moment he could do no wrong in Livi's eyes.

It's funny. For an easy-going guy, Jem can be quite persuasive.

Chapter 13

Tonight Jem's doing an extra shift in the hotel bar, which gives me time, at last, to catch up with Zoe. I'm looking forward to her coming round; it's been ages since we got together outside college. But as soon as she arrives, she starts getting on my nerves. She keeps on and on about how Jem never lets me out of his sight, till in the end I just want her to go. I've got too much I should be getting on with to listen to crap like that.

'What did you get for your *Hamlet* essay?' she asks, changing the subject at last.

'I haven't handed it in yet.'

'What?' She looks at me in horror, like I've planted a bomb in the student common-room or something.

'I haven't had time.'

'It's because you're always with Jem,' she says, returning to her well-worn theme. 'Tell him you've got work to do.'

'Jem doesn't stop me from working!' I snap, fed up with her now. She looks sceptical. 'He doesn't! He wants me to do well in my exams, if you must know. Then I can go to London and be with him.'

Zoe repeats my words slowly. 'He wants you to go to London?'

'Yes.'

'To be with him?'

'Yes.' What is wrong with her? She's making me uneasy.

'This is more serious than I thought!' Her face is a picture. 'He wants you to move in with him?'

'Yeah,' I say slowly. 'I guess so.'

Last night, when I was filling in my UCAS application Jem had said, 'Newcastle?' in surprise.

'What's wrong with Newcastle?'

'Nothing!'

'Jem?' I say warningly. We'd just been talking about how important it was to be honest and open with each other and now here he was, clamming up on me.

'OK. It's just that it's so far away. When will I get to see you?' He looks like a little kid.

I feel guilty. 'Oh, Jem, anywhere I go will be far away. But it's only term-time. We can see each other in the holidays.'

'The holidays,' he repeats, but he still looks miserable.

'And weekends. It's the north-east of England, not Outer Mongolia.'

But it might as well be, from his face. Then suddenly he stands up and hugs me to him, wrapping his arms around me in a stranglehold, like he'll never let me go.

'Come to London.' His voice in my ear is soft but compelling. 'We can be together all the time then.'

It seemed like a good plan. I was flattered to be asked, flattered he wanted me to share his London life with him, flattered he was thinking of us long-term.

And it would be so good to be together properly. Basically we had nowhere to go here. Nowhere to be alone. And I want to be alone with him, I really do.

So, filled with euphoria, I'd put down a London uni as my first choice and Newcastle as my insurance instead.

But now, all of a sudden, I'm nervous. Am I doing the right thing? Jem and me – it's brilliant. I'm so lucky I met him, I love him to bits. It's just that everything is moving so fast. Going to London to be with him is a huge commitment. One I now realize I haven't really thought through properly.

Zoe saying, 'He wants you to move in with him?' has panicked me. Because, when I agreed last night to go to London, I guess I still thought I'd be doing the whole uni experience I'd looked forward to for so long. Just not in Newcastle.

I'd thought there would still be:

A hall of residence.

A poky room with a desk and a single bed with my throw on it and my posters hiding the cracks in the walls.

Freshers' week.

Pub crawls.

Clubs.

Parties.

Late nights spent drinking too much.

Late mornings, with hangovers.

New mates.

No Mum. No Dad.

Freedom.

Only, now it wasn't going to be like that.

Because I'd be with Jem.

Zoe is still staring at me like I've grown two heads. I feel like saying to her, 'Leave me alone! I was all right with this until you started!'

But she beats me to it. She starts grabbing her things together and saying that she's got to go. Like we've had an argument. Like I've let her down or something.

Just who does she think she is?

I don't tell Jem any of this, of course. Soon I've got things more in perspective. It's not rocket science to work out I'm just a bit stressed out at the moment, what with the year I've had. Dad shacking up with Jude, me worrying all the time about Mum and what Livi's up to, stacks of college work to keep up with, Zoe being an idiot . . . What did I expect? No wonder I'm looking forward to getting away from this place, letting my hair down and having FUN!

And it's still going to happen. It is! Only it's going to be with Jem by my side.

Jem *is* fun. I'm discovering all the time there's loads more to him than meets the eye. He's not just attentive and considerate and drop-dead gorgeous and, of course, besotted with me (which, let's face it, is really what the problem with Zoe is – she's green with envy). He makes me laugh too – things he does, things he says. He's got a really quirky sense of humour once you get to know him. He's had some wicked things to say about Zoe (ha, ha) and some of my other friends. He thinks they're a bunch of losers, if the truth is known.

He's probably right.

I do want to be with Jem, I really do.

Stuff Zoe.

It had been a good night. He'd been spotted at one point under the bridge, he was sure of it, but he'd frozen into the shadows and the couple had walked on past. Wise move.

No one wanted to mess with a figure lurking in the dark on a cold winter's night. Goodness knows what he might be up to.

They'd find out soon enough.

Chapter 14

Jem and I are lying on my bed, facing each other, alone in the house for once. Mum's round Karen's and Livi's having a sleepover at a friend's.

I'm watching his mouth. It's a lovely mouth, full-lipped, clearly shaped. On one side the upper lip curls slightly. I trace the outline with my finger and he bites it gently.

'Love me?' he asks.

'Yes.'

'How much?'

'This much.' I kiss him and he kisses me back.

After a while I say, 'Do you love me?'

He looks down at me, his face so close to mine I can almost taste his sweet breath. 'What do you think?' he says and draws me into his arms.

I don't care about Dad and Jude.

I don't care about Zoe or exams or university or anything any more.

I just care about Jem.

An hour or so later, we are fast asleep in each other's arms when the front doorbell rings.

'Who's that?' I say, rising up on to my elbows.

'Don't worry about it,' says Jem, trying to pull me back down to him but it rings again. Then the letterbox rattles and a voice calls. 'Hello? Anyone at home?'

'It's my dad!' I sit bolt upright. 'Keep quiet. He should go away in a minute.'

But then there's the sound of a key in the lock. I jump out of bed, horrified, scrabbling for my clothes.

'Oh shit! He'll go ballistic!'

'Hello? Anyone there? Anna? Livi? Maggie?'

I thrust my legs into my jeans and chuck Jem his pants off the floor. 'Quick! Get dressed!'

'Anna? Is that you?'

'Be down in a minute, Dad.'

I finish dressing, run my fingers through my hair and hiss, 'Stay here till I get rid of him!' before I run downstairs.

He's in the kitchen, leaning against the worktop, arms folded.

'What are you doing here?' I say ungraciously. He looks at me strangely.

'Thought I'd try and catch you on the hop,' he says. 'Looks like I did.'

My hand goes to my hair, smoothing it down. 'What do you want?'

'To see you. You're hard to get hold of nowadays. Where's Livi?'

'At a sleepover.'

'Your mother?'

'Out. You should've called to let us know you were coming.'

He looks put out. 'I used to live here,' he reminds me.

'*Used* to,' I echo and busy myself making coffee. He follows me into the lounge where luckily my books are scattered all over the floor, where I'd left them when Jem came round.

'Revision?' he asks.

'Not yet. Still loads of work to do.'

'You're not slacking, are you?'

'No, I'm not slacking.'

'Only Jude said you were seeing someone.'

'Did she now?'

'James, is it?'

Huh? Oh yes, James who's at Oxford. James who's just

91

been shagging your daughter and is now hiding upstairs in her bedroom. I'd forgotten all about that little mix-up. I don't answer, mainly because I don't know what to say. I can feel him staring at me, dying to hear all about this elusive James.

'Still got your heart set on Newcastle?' he says, giving up.

'No. I've decided to go London now.'

'Why London?'

'Why not?'

He clicks his tongue, irritated. I'd never have got away with this level of rudeness if he was still living with us. But he'd forfeited any right to my respect when he'd left us to live with The Bitch in a Suit.

Though, it occurs to me, I still need him to pay my fees. And accommodation. And expenses. The whole lot, hopefully. So I add, 'I just changed my mind, Dad. People do. You should know that.'

He ignores my little barb. 'But that was the course you always wanted to do. You said it was the only one like it in the country. What do you want to go to London for? You won't like it there, Anna love, I'm telling you.'

'How do *you* know what I like and what I don't like?'

He looks hurt and I have to steel myself against him.

'I'm just concerned about you, that's all. You've been so set on Newcastle all along. We drove all the way up to have a look at the place, remember?'

Of course I remember. Vividly. It was the last time we went anywhere together as a family. It all floods back to me, how I felt at the time. Excited, elated, exuberant. I couldn't wait to get to Newcastle and live the student life.

'I remember that a week later you told us you were leaving us to live with Jude.'

Now he looks like I've slapped him in the face.

Don't do this to me, Dad. Don't make *me* feel guilty.

He sighs heavily. 'Well, it's your life. As long as you know what you're doing.'

'Do you?'

There's a cough at the lounge door. Jem is standing there. My heart sinks. What's he up to? I told him to stay upstairs.

'Who's this?' Dad frowns, first at Jem, then at me.

Jem comes forward. 'I'm—'

'James. This is James, Dad.'

Jem raises an eyebrow but rises to the occasion and extends his hand. 'Pleased to meet you.'

Dad shakes his hand, but the frown remains. 'James,' he says. 'You're at Oxford, I hear.'

Jem turns to me, puzzled. I give a little nod. 'That's right,' he says.

'What are you studying?'

'Medicine. He's studying Medicine. Aren't you, James?'

'Medicine. Yes. I'm studying Medicine.'

I can feel them both appraising each other carefully as we sit down together in the lounge, like a couple of stags, ready to lock horns.

Jem slips on to the sofa beside me, his arm resting possessively on my shoulders, which leaves Dad isolated in the armchair opposite us. Immediately he starts cross-examining Jem about Oxford and Medicine – of which, of course, Jem knows zilch. My heart sinks. He's so non-committal in his answers, he's coming across as rude.

I can feel Dad watching us all the time, watching Jem's hand with its distinctive tattoo stroking my arm, fiddling with my hair, even, at one point, absent-mindedly stroking my breast until, hot with embarrassment, I move to the edge of the seat. As the conversation dwindles, I become more and more tense and when Dad announces that he's going at last, it's all I can do not to jump up in relief.

Out in the hall, my father turns to me, his face serious. 'You do know what you're doing with him, don't you?'

'Of course I do!'

'Only—'

'Only what?' I sound defiant, even to me.

'He's older than you and—'

'A couple of years. You're twenty years older than Jude, in case you've forgotten.'

He nods, contrite. 'I know. But I'm not sure—'

'What's wrong, Dad? Is it the tattoo you don't like? Or the accent? Or the fact that someone actually wants to be with me?'

'Don't be silly. I just care about you, Anna, that's all. I don't want you to be hurt.'

'I'm not a kid any more. And Je— He's not going to hurt me, Dad. He loves me. And I love him.'

'I can see that,' says Dad. 'That's the trouble.'

He stares down at me, his eyes full of concern, and suddenly I don't want to argue with him any more, I just want him to put his arms round me and make it all better like he did when I was a kid. So I wrap my arms around his waist and press my face to his chest and he gives me a hug.

And I try not to cry.

When he's gone, I go back into the lounge. Jem is sitting with his feet up on the sofa, staring into the fire. I flop down beside him. He's as tight as a coiled spring.

'Why did you tell your father my name was James?' he asks.

'It was a mistake.'

'And I'm at Oxford? Studying Medicine. Was that a mistake too?

I groan.

'Are you ashamed of me?'

'NO!'

'Why then?'

'Because I'm an idiot,' I wail. 'Because I say the first thing that comes into my head. Because I was trying to impress his stupid girlfriend, if you must know.'

There's silence then he snorts derisively. 'You *are* an idiot. She doesn't deserve to be impressed.'

'I know! I'm sorry! I'm really sorry!' This is all going so wrong.

He's silent for a while. Then he says, 'I don't think your dad liked me very much.'

I don't think so either. But at least I manage not to say it out loud.

'He was surprised to see you, that's all. What did you come downstairs for? I asked you to stay in the bedroom.'

'I wanted to see what he was like.'

'And?'

He shrugs.

Great. My boyfriend and my father hate each other.

'You should have stayed upstairs,' I say regretfully. 'He's not daft, Jem. He knows we're sleeping together.'

Jem's beautiful mouth stretches into a pleased smile.

'Good,' he says and pulls me back into his arms.

The empty streets echoed with the rhythm of his pounding feet. He'd learnt how to deal with the rage that burnt within him on that course they'd sent him on last time. Part of the deal. Go on an anger management course and stay out of jail.

It was working. He was able to control his anger now. Most of the time. Keep it on pilot.

Until someone set it off again.

Chapter 15

Falling in love is everything I hoped it would be. Jem is the most sensitive, creative, romantic, original person I have ever come across in my whole life.

He is also the most deep and complex.

Every day I discover something new about him. He loves poetry, reading to me from Shakespeare and the Romantics and poets I never knew existed, even though I'm the one who's studying A-level English. Believe me, there is nothing more erotic than someone reading love poems to you in bed, even if the bed in question is in a poky hotel staff bedroom shared with others who could burst in on you at any moment.

He writes his own too – spare, bold verse, stripped of all pretence, that leaves me in no doubt about his feelings for me. He declares his love in striking, merciless rhyme:

I would go down for loving you.
But if I did, I'd bring you too.
And if you sent me down to hell
I'd take you with me there as well.

OK, I'm a Lit student and I recognize it may not be exactly the best poetry in the world. But, believe me, delivered in Jem's matter-of-fact monotone, it's powerful stuff. It's scary but humbling at the same time. He is so open, so trusting. For all he knows I could tread on his love, tear it to shreds, scatter it to the winds. Because he is so honest with me, I find myself opening up to him too. I write him poems back, laying bare my most passionate, private thoughts, for his eyes only.

He draws up a play list for me of his favourite songs and soon they become mine. I feel that he's educating me, taking me by the hand and leading me into his larger, more interesting world. He loves hip-hop, the urban raps which tell the story of real life on the streets. But then, paradoxically, this man of mine loves the song 'Vincent', which is a tribute to the brilliant, tortured artist Van Gogh, one of his idols. It's the sort of song my mum would like, sweet and schmaltzy, and I'm surprised by his choice. But then, as I listen to the haunting lyrics, his lonely soul possesses me too.

For they could not love you
But still your love was true

And when no hope was left in sight
On that starry, starry night.
You took your life
As lovers often do . . .

He takes me to an art gallery to see a Van Gogh exhibition, then to others, exposing me to new images and new ideas, from the beautiful to the bizarre.

He does drawings for me, and of me, quick, skilful illustrations, original and distinctive.

He takes photographs himself, all the time, of the docks, the city, people, things, but mostly of me. I'm his favourite subject, he's for ever clicking away when I least expect it. He must have hundreds of pictures of me. In some of them I'm posing for the camera, but in most I'm looking startled or caught unaware. On the wall above his bed in the hotel is a whole display of me getting on and off buses, bending over drying my hair, coming out of the loo, frowning with concentration, getting dressed, asleep with my mouth open, wrapped in a bath towel, laughing with friends.

Some I like. Some are not so flattering. One or

two, where too much flesh is showing or when I'm sleeping, are too intimate to be on display. They make me feel uncomfortable.

'Don't put those up!'

'Why not?' he says. 'You're beautiful,' and I grow bold in his approval. But later on when I see his room-mate eyeing the latest picture of me in my underwear I grow hot with shame and make him take them down.

Jem treats me like a queen, everyone says so. It's only Dad who's not so fussed.

And Zoe.

Zoe is being really weird about Jem. I think she's jealous. She's still single and she resents the time I spend with him. She had the cheek to tell me that she thinks he's too controlling. We've fallen out about it.

In fact she said more than that. It all started because she wanted me to go with her one night to see a band playing.

'I don't know . . .'

'You're going out with Jem,' she said, her voice flat. 'Of course. Stupid of me to ask.'

'Don't be like that!' I said in surprise. 'No, actually. It's because I don't like that band any more.'

'Why not?'

I shrugged. 'Moved on, I guess. I like other stuff now.'

'Stuff that Jem likes.' She sounded like she was sneering.

'Not necessarily. What are you trying to say?'

Jem says this, Jem thinks that, Jem likes this, Jem hates that.' Her voice, high and silly, parodied mine, stinging me to the quick. 'I'm sick of it, that's all.'

'Zoe!' I stared at her aghast. 'Jem doesn't tell me what to think.'

'You're joking! He's got inside your head, Anna! He controls you. Can't you see it?'

'Piss off!' I said, outraged, and she did.

We've hardly spoken since.

The thing is, she doesn't know Jem like I do. He comes across to her as brooding and intense, but there's loads more to him than meets the eye.

He's not just broadened my outlook on literature and music and art. He's introduced me to a whole new world I could never, ever tell her about.

She hasn't got a clue what we get up to when we're on our own.

And I'm not talking sex here. I'm talking street.

Jem has a secret.

Chapter 16

It turns out that Jem is not just a great photographer. He's a great artist as well. A graffiti artist. The best.

I guess I could have worked it out. He's Fin. His tag can be seen all over town. He's famous. Over the past few months he has stamped his personalized signature on buildings, trains, buses, walls, everywhere. Sometimes it appears on its own in the shape of a shark's fin; more often than not it is accompanied by an amazing illustration.

To some people he's a genius. To others he's a vandal. But no one can deny his talent. He is super-skilled and super-fast, time being of the essence. People write letters to the local newspaper about him; any new venture of his appears in its pages.

Actually, he's not just famous, he's infamous, because no one knows who Fin is. And that's the way Jem likes it. He has no interest whatsoever in revealing his identity, in 'coming out'. A big part of the buzz is in remaining anonymous, elusive, evading capture.

And all the time he leaves his mark on buildings that represent the establishment or the unacceptable face of capitalism. Schools, town halls, council offices, benefit agencies, the new Docklands development, even, to my own private amusement, the building which houses my father's brand-new apartment – all of them he has tagged. Sometimes he scrawls comments on them as well: terse, witty, subversive messages that provoke and undermine.

It's a big deal that he's told me. It's an even bigger deal that, more often than not, he takes me with him now. I've become his partner in crime.

His tag has changed. Fin no longer exists. Jem Smith has wrapped his arms around Anna Williams and together we have become JAWS. The signature resembles the wide

open mouth of a hungry Great White; the W of Williams,
a row of savage teeth.

Jem is teaching me everything he knows.

open mouth of a hungry Great White: the W of Williams;

a row of savage teeth.

Jenna teaching me everything he knows.

A girl and a boy together. Against the world.
Running through the night.
Stamping their signatures on public property.
Claiming it as their own.

Chapter 17

When I tell Mum I've changed my mind about uni and I'm going to London now to be with Jem, she's OK with it.

'It's closer than Newcastle,' she says, sounding pleased. 'I'm glad you're going to be with Jem, though. London's a big place. You could be very lonely there.'

Poor Mum. If anyone knows what it's like to be lonely, it's her. She doesn't go out much, except for work and her sad nights out with Karen. When she lost Dad, she lost their social life too. She's got a wardrobe full of posh frocks upstairs she hasn't put on since the day he left.

But when I tell her I'm thinking of studying Art instead of English, she's surprised.

'I thought you loved English?' she says.

'I do! But it's like Jem says, I'll read anyway, I don't need a degree to do that. Whereas, Art . . . there's more to it than just painting and drawing, you know. Jem says it's about expressing yourself, giving yourself a voice. I want to get into it, study it properly, find out about different artists, different periods, different methods . . .'

'Well, you certainly sound enthusiastic about it!' says Mum.

'I am. I'm serious, Mum. Jem and I have talked about it loads, and there's a great Art department at his college.'

'I don't believe it!' breathes Livi. 'You're going to London to be with Jem. That is so romantic!'

Mum looks at me, concerned. 'Well, you've always been such a sensible girl, I'm sure you know what you're doing. Your father's not going to like it though.'

She's right. My father goes ballistic.

'*Art?*' he says, like I've said I'm going to study party games or joined-up writing. 'That's not a subject.'

'Of course it is.'

'Not a proper subject. You don't even have to go to university to study it.'

'I'm not going to uni any more. I'm going to college.'

'College?' He looks as if he's going to explode. 'Over my dead body.'

'Don't tempt me,' I mutter.

'Which college is it?'

I tell him.

'Never heard of it.'

'It's got a great reputation.'

'What for? Drugs? Anarchy? The number of students who drop out?'

'If you're going to be childish I'm not going to talk to you. It's a good college.'

'Who says?'

I don't say anything.

'Oh, I get it.' His mouth curls up into a particularly unattractive sneer. 'It's him, isn't it? The boyfriend. He's the one who's pulling your strings.'

'Nobody's pulling my strings,' I protest, my face aflame.

'I can see it, Anna, even if you can't. He's in Oxford, you're in London. Bit closer than Newcastle, isn't it? He can keep an eye on you there.'

I'd forgotten Dad thought James-not-Jem was at Oxford. If he found out Jem-not-James was in London, he'd go totally ape-shit.

'He's got you exactly where he wants you!' he says bitterly. I don't deign to reply. 'What does your mother think of this idea?' he adds.

'She's fine with it.'

'She would be. She doesn't understand the opportunities you're throwing away.'

I stare at him in disbelief. He knows all about opportunities all right.

Golden Boy. Scholarship to grammar school, a university degree, a career in law. Somewhere along the way he'd returned to marry the pretty girl-next-door, who'd been waiting patiently for him. She'd stayed at home and brought up the kids, he'd worked his way up to senior partner. Perfect arrangement. Till he dumped her for Golden Girl.

I'd hated him for updating my mother for a newer, streamlined model. But until this moment I'd never thought he was ashamed of the old one.

'*She doesn't understand . . .* How patronizing is that?'

He has the grace to look embarrassed. 'I didn't mean it like that.'

'Yes you did!' I let him see how angry I am. Because it makes him feel bad. And because it distracts him from the effect his words have had upon me.

Deep down I know I'm throwing away my dream. I don't need anyone to point this out to me, least of all my father. But it's too late now to do anything about it. I'm miles behind with my work and I'm never going to get the grades I need to do English at Newcastle anyway.

I want to get away. I'm not hanging around here for another year to watch my father fawning over The Bitch, my mother fading away and my sister making a fool of herself, while Zoe zooms off to uni and Jem goes back to college without me.

And Jem's suggestion of studying Art – it's a great idea. A gateway into a whole new world. Art is so much more than conventional painting and drawing. It's about exposing yourself to whole new cultures.

Like graffiti for example.

Jem says, it's not just an art form, it's an attitude.

And now I'm with him, I'm discovering I've got plenty of that.

The anger was bubbling up inside him again. She belonged to him. What right did that tosser have to steal her away?

It was all his fault he was stuck here like this in this half-life. Neither here nor there. Just watching and waiting for her to get tired of the idiot and notice him again.

Well, he was getting fed up with it. There was a limit even to his patience.

Chapter 18

Despite my good intentions, I allow my father to get to me. It's not surprising really, he won't let up. He takes me out for a meal to a posh restaurant and tries to convince me over four courses and two bottles of wine that I'm making a big mistake.

It's like it's a personal affront to him that I've deviated from the grand plan. At one point he even says to me, 'Jude thinks this is your way of punishing me for being with her,' and I snap, 'This is not about you, Dad! It's about me!' I'm furious at the thought of The Bitch and him discussing me in such a condescending way like I'm a child who's spat the dummy out of the pram. What does *she* know? She's only a few years older than me!

He runs through all the doors a university degree will open for me and I refuse to rise to the bait until he dares to use *her* as an example of where I want to be in ten years' time.

'Think about it, Anna. You could be like Jude. Educated, qualified, on an upward career path . . .'

'. . . and sleeping with the boss, who's twice my age?'

Dad's face flushes an ugly shade of purple and I feel a prick of triumph. At last I've got to him. He fizzles out after that and I'm left feeling oddly disappointed. And mean. I'm so glad when my phone bleeps. Dad raises his eyebrows.

'James?'

'Um . . . yes.'

'I'll get the bill.'

He knows when he's beaten.

Jem wants to know when I'll be free. I text him back that I'll meet him outside the bank in ten minutes.

Dad flips his card on the plate without bothering to see how much it is. I guess it doesn't matter when it's all on expenses. He pours more wine into his glass without offering me any.

'Can I book you a taxi home?' he asks politely, like he would to a very junior colleague.

'No thanks. I'm meeting—'

'James. I thought you would be.' He takes out his phone and calls a taxi for himself. It's like he doesn't care any more. He just wants to get home. To her.

We sit there in silence like two strangers. We've got nothing else to say to each other.

I *want* to say something to him. I want to say, 'Don't give up on me, Dad. Don't stop caring about me. You see, it's not as easy as you think, it's not a straightforward choice. The truth is, I don't know what I want. I think I do when I'm with Jem. But sometimes, when I'm alone, I can see what Zoe means when she says he's controlling. I love him, I really do, but he can be quite persuasive, in the nicest possible way, of course. I don't quite know how he does it . . .'

That's what I *want* to say. Instead I say, 'Dad?' and he looks up at me and says, 'Yes?' and at last we connect. I open my mouth to speak to him properly, to tell him all this stuff that's tearing me apart, and then a voice says, 'Anna? Are you ready?' and Jem is standing in front of me.

'What are you doing here?' I ask blankly and he says, 'I saw you through the window.'

'Don't let me keep you,' says Dad and he gets to his feet. 'My taxi's here.' He gives me a peck on the cheek, then he's gone.

Jem flops down into his vacant seat and picks up the bottle of wine. 'Shame to waste it,' he says and pours us both a glass. 'Did you have a good time?'

Now Dad's gone, I offload on to Jem instead. I don't tell him my doubts about going to London with him. Instead I focus on Jude and how much I loathe her. Jem is a great listener. He calls for another bottle of wine and, fuelled by it, we spend a bitter-sweet half-hour pulling her apart, even though he's never met her.

'I hate her, I really do,' I rant. 'Waltzing into our lives like that, breaking up our home.'

'Bitch,' agrees Jem companionably.

'She is a bitch! She's totally vile. She told my dad I'm only going to London with you just to get at him.'

'You're not, are you?'

'No, of course not. She's just an . . .'

'Evil bitch.'

'Exactly. If you met her you'd think butter wouldn't melt in her mouth, but she's a right cow, she's a liar and a cheat and she sees what she wants and just takes it, and she doesn't give a stuff about anyone else . . .'

I continue ranting and raving, hardly pausing to take a breath, and Jem continues nodding and listening patiently without interrupting, except to insert the odd expletive that seems to encapsulate Jude perfectly.

At last I run out of steam and he takes my hand. 'Better now?'

'Not really.' I hiccup sadly. 'I hate her.'

'I think I've got that.'

'I hate him too.' I don't actually mean that, but it gives me a certain satisfaction to say it.

'So?' He raises my hand to his lips and kisses my fingers, one by one, his eyes locked into mine. It's mesmerizing. 'Do something about it then.'

'Like what?'

He doesn't answer. Instead he gives me that wicked smile of his. I feel myself coming alive again.

'Have you got any with you?'

He taps his pocket. I jump to my feet.

'Let's go then. What are we waiting for?'

As we head out of the door, the waiter calls, 'Excuse me, sir, madam. Would you like to settle your bill?'

For a second I'm puzzled.

'The wine,' says Jem quietly and turns to the waiter.

'No thanks,' he says politely. 'Put it on the big-shot lawyer's account instead. He can afford it.' Then he grabs my hand and together we make a bolt for it down the road, laughing, and jump on the first bus we can find heading for the docks.

That is the first time I have ever run out of somewhere without paying. I feel elated, like I'm high on drugs. I feel invincible. On the top deck we snog fiercely, all over each other, regardless of the other passengers. I don't know what's got into me. I want to do it here, right now, on top of the bus. But Jem is on the move again, pulling me up out of the seat. We're already there.

When the bus moves off, we're left alone in the darkness, with just the boats knocking forlornly together and the sea lapping up against the harbour wall for company. Across the road looms the apartment block, some of its windows shrouded in curtains or blinds, others blazing with light. I tip my head back and gaze up at the top storey. Someone is gazing out over the sea. It's Jude. My father comes into view and wraps his arms round her. They kiss. I turn to Jem, unable to watch any more. He's watching them too, his expression tense, raw.

He takes the spray cans out of his pocket and hands one to me, and without a word we run across the road and get to work.

Chapter 19

It was totally awesome up on the roof of Wharfside. You could see for miles.

Jem helped me climb up there via neighbouring buildings, up and up till we reached the top. It was easier than I thought. It was so high up I was too scared to look down at first. But after a while I got used to it. I wouldn't hang over the edge to write on the wall though. I hung on to Jem's legs for grim death while he did it instead.

When he'd told me what he'd written, I was crying laughing. He'd sprayed *The Bitch* and *Her Keeper* above their massive front window.

After that it becomes a bit of a habit. An addiction. I start to need a regular fix. It's the adrenalin rush, the playing with fire, never knowing if you're going to get caught. Jem combines graffiti with free-running. He is ace at it, leaping, vaulting, pushing against walls with his feet, propelling himself up them. He's like a cat, strong and supple, and makes it look so easy. I'm useless compared to him.

We spend more and more nights together, tagging around the town. By the time I meet up with Jem after he's finished work, there's hardly a soul about. No one knows what I'm up to.

Mum thinks I'm revising in my room. When she takes herself off for her early nights in her lonely bed, I'm hard at it, swotting for my exams.

I wish! I can't remember when I last did any work for college. I can't seem to settle to anything. Since I started tagging, I feel like I'm in a permanent state of heightened alert. Plus I'm knackered because I'm out half the night.

Livi knows I go AWOL once Mum is safely tucked up in bed, but she thinks I'm nipping out to be with Jem. Which I am, only not in the way she presumes. And she's never going to split on me. Because she idolizes Jem. Plus, I cover up for her all the time. She's still hanging out with the wrong crowd, acting like a little tramp and pining for that little rat, Ferret.

Idiot! I blame my dad for her bad taste in men. I mean, what sort of male role model has she got to aspire to? It's lucky Jem's around to show her not all men are shits.

Jem and I have become more and more creative. We

used to just leave our tag. Then we got clever with stencils and did some nice quick designs of sharks with their jaws open wide. We got into the local paper with those. It was surprising how many people actually liked them, especially the ones on the wall of the council swimming pool.

But lately we've been leaving messages, ever since we wrote on the wall of Dad's apartment. It takes more time, obviously, but it's worth it for the buzz. Jem is brilliant at thinking up phrases. Once he wrote *Not in use* on the front of a bus. I nearly died laughing, thinking how many times I'd been caught out like that.

Last week he wrote *No alcohol* on the front door of his hotel. Then we climbed over the gate into the railway station and I wrote *No waiting* on the waiting room, which was risky because it's CCTVed, but that's what gives you the thrill.

The next night we went out again and inscribed *Private, Keep Out!* all over the front of the posh girls' school on the outskirts of town. We nearly got caught that night by a stupid caretaker and we had to run for our lives through the bushes. I was scratched to bits. It was such a high. We ended up going back to Jem's and tearing each other's clothes off. It turns you on when you think you're about to get caught but you get away with it.

* * *

Tonight we are heading into town. To be honest, I'm not really in the mood.

Yesterday Dad had let drop that he was away next week in New York with The Bitch.

'Supposed to be a business trip,' he'd said, looking very pleased with himself. 'But actually, Jude's looking forward to doing some early Christmas shopping in Times Square.'

Smug, smarmy swine.

'I can't afford to do Christmas shopping in Lidl!' said Mum bitterly.

I was so mad at him.

When I told Jem he'd curled his lip and said, 'All right for some. That's why lawyers charge such high fees. Because their girlfriends are such high maintenance.'

Then today, Zoe asked me to go to the cinema with her and I was thrilled because I thought she'd been avoiding me, so I said yes without thinking and she looked chuffed to bits. Then Jem called me and he was really moody and said he had something special planned for us and in the end I gave in. Zoe was furious . . .

Jem won't tell me what he's got in mind. He likes keeping me in suspense.

'This is where my dad's office is,' I say when we get off the all-night bus and head round the corner.

Jem treats me to his lopsided grin.

'Oh, no!' The penny drops. 'Not again!'

After we'd sprayed the front wall of Dad's flat, I'd spent days petrified he'd work out it was us.

'Why would he?' said Jem. He was right, of course. We never heard a thing about it.

Jem can be pretty persistent when he wants to be. He's like a dog with a bone. When he's got his teeth into something, he won't give it up. 'First his flat,' he says. 'Then his workplace. Maybe this time he'll get the message.'

'No way!'

'Come on, Anna.' Jem's eyes flash with sudden anger. 'He deserves it. So does she. Look how they treated you girls and your mum. You can't expect to treat people like shit and get away with it.'

I bite my lip. He had a point. 'OK. But nothing personal, right?'

'Right.'

Tonight I stand and watch as he sprays paint in large letters on the front door of Williams & Barnes. I've got to admit, he's got a way with words. I can't help laughing as the message appears.

Lawyers suck . . . you dry

I add our tag with a flourish, making the W on JAWS just a tad more vicious-looking than normal.

'OY! What the hell do you think you are doing?'

A torch beams straight into my eyes and I nearly jump out of my skin. Behind it I can just make out the bald head and bright-green day-glo jacket of a security guard. I stand there trapped in the glare like a rabbit caught in headlights.

From behind me there's a sudden movement and something shoots straight past me at high speed like a bullet from a gun. The guy roars and falls to his knees, holding his face in his hands. There's blood everywhere. I scream.

Then Jem grabs my hand and we're running, running, running. Only this time, nobody's laughing.

Silly bitch. Screaming enough to waken the dead.
Must've thought they'd killed the guy.
You need to toughen up a bit, sunshine.
Get real.

Chapter 20

'No! No! No! No!' We turn the corner before I come to my senses and, using both hands and all my weight, manage to drag Jem to a standstill. 'Go back! We've got to go back!' I plead with him desperately. 'You might have killed him!'

His face twists into a delighted grin.

'It's not funny!' I screech at him. 'What's wrong with you? He could be bleeding to death!'

'It's paint, Anna. I sprayed paint at him.'

I stare at him blankly.

'What? You think I *shot* him?'

My eyes close and I collapse against him, my face against his chest. His arms go around me briefly, then he says, 'Come on. We can't hang around here. There'll be someone here in a minute. He'll be on his radio.'

'Will he be all right?' I say reluctantly, looking back,

and he says, 'Yes!' Then there's the unmistakable wail of a police siren and I am about to make a bolt for it in blind panic when he says, 'Stop!' and grabs my beanie from my head so my hair tumbles down to my shoulders. He pulls his off too, stuffing them both into his pocket, and puts his arm around me.

'Put yours round me too,' he instructs. 'And your head on my shoulder. That's it. Now walk with me slowly, *slowly* . . . keep your face turned into me . . .'

To my surprise he turns around and we're walking back the way we've come, a parody of a loving couple strolling into town on an innocent night out, just as a police car tears up behind us. We watch as it screams past round the corner, then he turns around again, grabs my hand and we leg it as fast as we can in the other direction.

I have *never* been so scared in all my life.

Chapter 21

On Wednesday evening a security guard was attacked in Broadfield Road.

Peter Jones, aged 46, had paint sprayed in his face when he surprised two youths daubing slogans on the wall of Williams & Barnes solicitors. Jones was later released from hospital and is recovering at home.

Police are investigating the incident.

'That's your dad's place isn't it? Williams & Barnes?'

'Yeah.'

'You never said!'

I shrug. 'Nothing to say.'

'What? Your dad's office gets graffitied and a guy gets attacked and it's not worth mentioning?'

'I forgot.'

We're in the common-room at college, eating lunch.

Zoe's reading the paper. She's so flipping loud people come over to see what the fuss is about. Great. The next minute there's a small crowd gathered round reading the article, including Ben and Max.

'That's that *Jaws* guy, I bet,' says know-all Max. 'You see his stuff everywhere.'

'It's Anna's dad's office,' repeats Zoe.

There's a buzz of excitement. I could kill her.

'What did he write on it, Anna?'

'Dunno.'

'Bet your dad was mad.'

'Maybe. I don't talk to my dad if I can help it.'

I can feel Zoe watching me. She knows that is not exactly true.

'Urban shark, that's what they call him.'

'Respect.'

'Respect?' says Zoe, on her high horse. 'I don't think so. He attacked an innocent man.'

'It was just paint,' I say quietly.

'So?' She turns on me immediately. 'Would you like to have paint sprayed in your face? It's toxic, you know. There's lead and all sorts in it. He could've been blinded.'

'It's not toxic.' This is exactly what I'd said to Jem. He'd told me it wasn't nowadays. But I'd looked it up online

138

to double-check. 'They released him as soon as they'd cleaned him up.'

'How do you know?' asks Ben.

'What?' He's caught me off guard. 'It says here.'

'It says he's *recovering*. Which means he's getting better. Which means he must have been in a bad way.'

I feel sick. I hadn't thought of it like that. Ben's so nice. I think he's wrong, I think it's just a phrase the papers use, but I can't be sure.

'This guy is the king,' insists Max.

'The king?' says Zoe.

'He's the best, man. You don't get it, do you?' Max smiles down at her in that annoyingly superior way he has that she couldn't see when she was going out with him, even though she has a million more brain cells that he has. I think she sees it now.

'No,' she says, her voice ominously quiet. 'Tell me about it.'

Max rolls his eyes. 'It's political, innit?'

'Political?'

'Yeah, man. He's anti all this capitalist rubbish. Bankers and lawyers and that. He's making a protest.'

'About what?'

'You know. Stuff. People who make too much money. Rich people who rip the poor off.'

'The poor?'

'Yeah. Ordinary people like you and me.'

'You? Poor?'

'Yeah.'

'You in your designer trainers and designer jeans?'

Everyone laughs. Max goes red. 'Shut your face! Everyone has this stuff. It doesn't mean anything. I don't care about it.'

'Don't you?' There's a gleam in her eyes. She picks up her yoghurt and peels the top off. Oh no. 'You sure about that?'

'Yeah.'

With a flick of her wrist, yoghurt shoots out of the pot. Max yelps and jumps backwards, but he's not quick enough and the yoghurt lands squarely on his crotch and drips down his legs. A cheer goes up around the common-room.

'Oops, sorry about that,' she says with a grin. 'Just think of it as a political protest.'

Max backs away, cursing and swearing, dabbing ineffectually at his jeans as all his mates roll about with laughter. Zoe grins at me cheerfully.

'He had that coming to him. Waste of good yoghurt though.'

She looks so pleased with herself I can't help grinning

back. 'Um? Remind me? What's the difference between throwing paint and throwing yoghurt at someone?'

'Yoghurt tastes better. I waited a long time for that.'

'Revenge is sweet.' We smile at each other in satisfaction. But then, stupidly, I can't resist adding, 'You've got to admit it though, he's got a point.'

She shakes her head impatiently. 'That tosser doesn't know what he's talking about. He's just reciting garbage he's heard other people saying.'

'These graffiti artists,' I persist. 'This guy, JAWS. He's making a political statement.'

'Is he? And there's me thinking he's just a sad loner with no one to talk to. So he writes up his thoughts for all the world to see instead. But nobody cares . . .'

'I care!' I say, but she rants on regardless.

'. . . plus, he's not quite brave enough to use his own name.'

'Rubbish!' I spring automatically to Jem's defence. 'He's amazing! He's anti-authority. He's fighting against the establishment . . . against consumerism. He cares about people . . . about society. He's a rebel. An urban terrorist.'

'Yeah? So why doesn't he come right out and say who he is then? Put his money where his mouth is. Osama Bin Laden – we all know his name, don't we?'

I could scream with frustration. Zoe is so hard to beat in an argument.

'Because he's *not* an egotist, that's the point. He doesn't want to be in the limelight. It's what he believes in that's important, not notoriety.'

Where did I pluck that word from? I'm pleased with it though because it shuts Zoe up at last. Then I realize she is staring at me, wide-eyed.

'You seem to know a lot about him.'

'So?' My heart starts to beat rapidly. Me and my big mouth. We'd be in big trouble, if anyone found out. 'You can't help knowing about him. He's everywhere. He's on my dad's flat, my dad's office.'

'I know.' Her eyes narrow suspiciously. 'Why would you stick up for someone who scrawls stuff about your dad?'

'Because it's true,' I say bitterly. 'Lawyers *do* earn too much, everyone knows that. My dad's got money coming out of his ears. He's taking The Bitch to New York, Christmas shopping.'

She looks at me, her face blank.

'Anyway, it's not personal,' I backtrack. 'This guy doesn't know my dad. He just hates lawyers in general. I guess.'

Still she says nothing.

'I don't know!' I say wildly. 'I don't know the first thing about him, I'm just . . . speculating! I don't even know if it *is* a him, come to that. It could be a her. It could be more than one person. It could be anybody!'

Zoe's eyes look as if they're about to pop out of her head.

'Now,' she says, 'you are really freaking me out!'

On the whole he was pleased with the way things were going.

Couldn't afford to get complacent though.

You never knew where you were with women.

But he knew how to handle them.

They were putty in his hands.

Chapter 22

Mum and Livi think the sun shines out of Jem. It's quite the norm for me to come home from college to find Jem laid out on the sofa, drinking coffee and chatting away to one or the other. I swear he talks more to them than he does to me! Livi hangs on to his every word and sometimes I think Mum's just as bad.

Our house has become his second home. Let's face it, it's much nicer than his *first* home, the manky staff hotel room he shares with two other guys.

But that's not technically his first home, is it? When he's in London he lives in a bedsit. I think. Though even that's not his real home.

Actually, where does he go when it's not term-time? Why don't I know that?

Not for the first time it strikes me how little I actually know about Jem. When we'd talked, that first night on the boat, he'd poured his heart out to me and I'd thought how open and honest he was.

He told me he'd been hurt in the past and that's why he'd backed off. He was scared to commit again – and I couldn't blame him. A whole catalogue of women had let him down, starting with his mum and ending with his last girlfriend, who'd gone off with some older guy.

But it was no good. He couldn't stop thinking about me.

I was so flattered.

But since then, I really haven't found out that much more about his background. He's a dark horse, my boyfriend.

Where are you from, Jem? I wonder. Who are you? Where do you call home? So I ask him and he looks surprised, then he does that annoying thing of tapping his nose and winking at me. 'Wouldn't you like to know?' he says.

'Yes. I would, actually.'

'All in good time,' he says infuriatingly. So I tickle him and he's roaring laughing, but he still won't give. 'I'm your mystery man,' he says. 'It's part of my charm.'

'I'll find out!' I warn him but he just laughs.

Then he kisses me and I don't care any more.

On the evenings Jem's not at work, he eats with us

now. He always thanks Mum politely for his meal.

'What a nice boy!' I hear her sighing to herself as we go up to my bedroom after dinner one night. I smile to myself. He's got her wound round his little finger – she's already planning what she's going to feed him tomorrow night. Actually, if you think about it, he's probably the first person in a long while who hasn't taken Mum for granted. He thinks she's ace and the feeling is mutual.

Upstairs, Jem waxes lyrical about my mum's cooking, I tease him about it.

'I'm starting to think you're in love with my mother, you go on about her so much.'

His face breaks into a smile. 'Oh no, you've discovered my secret! Say what you like about your father, he does have impeccable taste in women.'

'He went off with The Bitch, let me remind you!' I explode and dive on him. We are rolling over and over on the floor, playfighting, and then we are kissing, touching . . .

And the door opens and Livi walks in.

'Oops! Sorry!' she says and backs out quickly. Jem groans with frustration and I sit up and pull my top back down.

'This is doing my head in!' I say through clenched teeth. 'We are never on our own in this place.'

149

'We need to find somewhere we can be alone together.'

Downstairs the phone rings. I can hear Mum answering it and then she calls up the stairs, her voice sounding a bit strange. 'Anna? Olivia? Someone wants a word with you!'

'Who?' I yell down but she doesn't answer. I disentangle myself from Jem, who is still lying on the floor, and go downstairs.

When I come back up, I'm in an even worse mood.

'What's up?' asks Jem.

'Guess who it was? The Bitch!'

He sits up. 'What did she want?'

'They're off to New York tomorrow, shopping. She wanted to know what we wanted from *them* for Christmas.'

'Kind of her.'

'Cow! I don't want anything from *her*. She's just rubbing it in. I feel like going down there now and writing all over her wall: *Jude is an evil bitch*. I don't think she got the message last time.'

'Can do. Just wait till they're safely tucked up in bed. Better still, wait till tomorrow when they're in mid-air over the Atlantic and you can write what you like. How long are they going for?'

'I dunno. Three nights, maybe four.'

'Plenty of time.' His face takes on a dark, brooding

quality that I've seen so many times before when he's deep in thought. He knows how much I hurt inside. Then all of a sudden his expression changes, like a light has switched on inside his head.

'What is it?'

'Problem solved!' He throws his arms around me, squeezing me so tight I can hardly breathe. 'Don't you see?'

'See what?'

'We've found our place to be alone!'

'You don't mean . . . ?'

'Your dad's flat. It's perfect! It's going to be empty and you've got a key!'

'I dunno . . .'

'Anna, come on! It's not like we're breaking in or anything.' Jem's eyes are shining with excitement. 'We're just taking over an unoccupied building for a while. Squatters' rights. It's perfectly legal.'

'Four days on our own.' It is so tempting.

'And four nights!' His eyes soften and he picks up my hand and kisses it. 'Anna, I can't believe it, it's the answer to our prayers. We can be together all night long.'

'Jem, I can't . . . Mum will be asking questions if I disappear for that long . . .'

'Don't worry.' He kisses me – a long, unhurried kiss.

'We'll work something out.' His lips move down to my throat. 'We've got all the time in the world.'

Almost where he wanted to be.

Not with who he wanted to be with.

But he was getting there.

One step at a time.

Chapter 23

The next day at college I can hardly contain my excitement. I'm going to meet Jem after work and, if we feel like it, we're going out tagging. Then it's back to Dad's.

I'm elated, but scared.

In my free period I go down to the library to try to get some work done. I'm so behind it's difficult to know where to start. I need to revise for a test in Sociology but I'm missing half the notes. I bow my head and read over what I've got, trying to fight down a rising feeling of panic. I'm never going to pass.

'Hi.'

I look up. Zoe's standing in front of me.

'Hi.'

There's an awkward silence. We've hardly spoken since the incident in the common-room. She's a bright girl, Zoe. I was afraid she'd found us out but she'd never mentioned it.

'What you up to?'

'Revising. We've got a test next lesson, haven't we?'

She nods, eyeing my thin file dubiously. I close it with a thump. 'There's no point, I've missed too much.'

'Borrow mine,' she says and she hands me her file. 'I'm up to date.'

'Thanks.' I smile at her gratefully. 'You're a life-saver.' She smiles back.

'Look,' she says. 'Why don't you come round to mine tonight after college?'

I hesitate.

'Sorry. Silly me. You're busy,' she says, her voice clipped, and turns away. I don't want her to go.

'No, wait!' I'm trying to work it all out in my head. Jem's going to work straight through today, he won't be waiting for me at home. I could do it. I could go home with Zoe then nip back to mine to change and pick up my stuff and meet him as planned after work. I come to a decision.

'That would be great, Zo, I'd love to.'

Her face lights up in surprise. 'Brilliant! We can go out if you want? Or get takeaway? Whatever you want.'

'Fine. I just need to phone to say what I'm doing.'

'Jem?' Her smile turns into a scowl. 'He'll talk you out of it.'

'No he won't! Anyway, it's my mum I have to ring, not him.

She has the grace to look embarrassed. 'Sorry. It'll be great to catch up. It's been ages.'

Damn right it has. Too late I remember I've been deliberately keeping my distance from Zoe since the newspaper incident. But it looks as if she's forgotten all about it.

'Better get on with my work,' I say, indicating the file. 'Thanks for the notes.'

I start working my way through them but it's like wading through treacle. I've missed too much. I'll never catch up.

My tutor thinks so too. At the end of the test he flicks through the meagre pages I hand in, his lips pursed.

'Maybe you should consider dropping Sociology, Anna, and concentrate on your other subjects,' he says, in front of everyone. My cheeks flame as the others exchange startled glances. Hypocrite! His voice is full of oily concern but all he cares about is his exam results.

The day goes from bad to worse. In English, where I thought I'd been more or less keeping up, Mrs Hopkins, my favourite teacher and my personal tutor, tells me my latest essay is not up to its usual standard. In French I get into trouble for not handing in my work. When I walk into the Art room, my Art teacher pretends to do a double-take. 'How nice to see you, Miss Williams! We'd thought you'd left the country. Blah, blah, blah-de-blah . . .' I walk straight back out again. I can't take much more of this.

I'd have gone home, only I'd promised Zoe I'd wait for her, so I hang around in reception. Wrong move. Mrs Hopkins comes past and stops when she sees me.

'Everything all right, Anna?'

'Fine.'

'Good. Only, I've just had a word with Mr Hall. He tells me he's advised you to drop Sociology.'

Blimey, he didn't waste much time! 'Yes. It's probably a good idea.'

'Is anything wrong, dear? The thing is, Madame Cassian says that you're struggling with French too.'

'No. I've just fallen behind a bit, that's all.'

Her kind, round face is full of concern. 'You're such a talented girl, but A levels are hard work. I have to admit even in English, I've noticed that your heart isn't in it any more.'

She looks so sad, I deny it fiercely. 'I love English! It's just that I've got a lot on at the moment . . .'

'Would you like to talk about it? I'm sure we could find some way to help you organize your time better . . .'

I wish. My phone rings. It's Jem. 'Not now. I can't . . .'

She pats me lightly on the arm. 'Come and see me tomorrow, morning break. We'll have a chat. See if I can help.'

I nod blindly, her kindness making me want to cry, and watch her back view waddling away down the corridor.

'How you doing?' says Jem's voice.

'Terrible,' I say flatly. 'I'm in trouble with everyone. English, French, Sociology, Art. The lot. I might as well give up now.'

There's silence on the other end. Then he says, 'Maybe that's not such a bad idea.'

'What?' I wasn't expecting that. I was hoping for a bit of encouragement.

'Pack it in. Who needs a degree anyway? All you'll get is a headache, a massive debt and no job at the end of it.'

'But I thought you wanted me to come to London with you?' I say in surprise.

'I do. Of course I do. But you don't have to go to uni to do that. Get a job. Live off the state. University isn't the only option.'

I swallow. It was for me. It was my dream.

Was.

I watch my dream mutate and disappear.

English degree in Newcastle.

English degree in London college.

Art degree in London college

Any sort of degree in any sort of college . . .

A vision of me telling my father I'd changed my mind again about my future passes before my eyes. *It's OK, Dad, I've seen the light. I'm not going to that obscure college of higher education to study Art after all. I'm going to sell* The Big Issue *on Oxford Street instead.*' My father had very strong views indeed about what he referred to as 'The Benefit Society'. He would probably have a heart attack.

'Look, we'll talk about it later. Don't worry about it.' His voice, calm and even, riles me. He has no idea. 'Are you on your way home now?'

'No, I'm going to Zoe's.'

There's silence at the end of the phone. 'I thought we were meeting up?' His voice is altered now, accusatory.

'We are! But not till you finish work.'

'Well make sure you're not late then.'

My temper flares. 'Don't talk to me like that! I've had a shit day, Jem. I don't need this!'

Silence.

And then the phone goes dead.

Spoilt bitch. Always wanting her own way.

He was too nice, that was his trouble. Too nice for his own good.

Maybe it was time to teach her a lesson.

Chapter 24

It's good to be at Zoe's again. She lives in one of those tall, draughty, Victorian terraces and I'd forgotten how much I love spending time here. Tonight we've got the house to ourselves. They've an open fire and we end up making mountains of toast, blackened and burnt but dripping with butter, and totally delicious. We wash it all down with mugs of strong, sweet tea. Mine comes in the Best Friend mug I'd bought Zoe for her twelfth birthday.

'Just what I needed,' I say with satisfaction, placing the empty mug down beside me. 'Aahh. Can't believe you've still got this old thing.'

'Of course! I'm still your BFF, aren't I?'

'You bet!' I grin at her. I don't know what I'd do without Zoe. We've been through everything together. School, college, periods; first bras, first dates, first loves. We'd shared our hopes, our dreams, our innermost thoughts.

Nobody knew me as well as Zoe.

Until now.

She smiles back at me. 'You OK, Anna?'

Suddenly I want to tell her. Everything. I want to say I'm worried sick because Jem and I have had a row. I want to say he rang me straight back but I turned my phone off because I need time to think. I want to say that this relationship with Jem, it's amazing, but it's running away with me, it's all going too fast. It's taking me places I'm not sure I want to go . . .

'Why does everyone keep asking me if I'm OK?' I say, but it comes out wrong. I sound irritable.

'Because they're worried about you?'

'I'm fine.'

'You're not fine. Ever since . . .' She pauses.

'Ever since what?' But I know what she's going to say.

'Ever since you've been going out with Jem, you've not been yourself.' It comes out in a rush.

Why did I think I could talk to her? She doesn't like Jem. I stare at her balefully.

'Don't be ridiculous. Who have I been then?'

'I don't know! Someone different. Someone I don't recognize,' she says wildly.

'What do you mean?'

164

'You're always at his beck and call, Anna. He's for ever ringing you, checking up on you, keeping tabs on what you're doing.'

'He's not ringing me now, is he?' I say triumphantly. Got her! 'Anyway, he is my boyfriend. That's what people do when they're going out together. Look what you were like with Max.'

'I know. That's the point. I was besotted with him. I couldn't see what a loser he was . . .'

'Jem's not a loser!'

'I never said he was! But you've changed, Anna, admit it. It's like he's taken you over; all you ever think about is him. You're not getting your work done, you're knackered all the time . . .'

'Who are you, my mother? And she really likes him, by the way.'

'Yeah, but she doesn't know what you're up to with him, night after night, does she?'

'What we get up to is our business!'

'I'm not talking sex, Anna!' she says, her cheeks aflame.

I stare at her, horrified. Zoe knows. She knows that we're JAWS.

She tries again, voice gentler now, her hand on my arm.

165

'Anna, I care about you . . .'

I shake it off, leaping to my feet.

'No you don't, you're jealous.'

'Jealous?'

'Yeah! Because I've got someone and you haven't.'

She stares at me, the colour draining from her face. She'd had sex, once, with Max, and then he'd left her. She'd felt used, abandoned. I was the only one who knew.

'That's not fair . . .'

'*You're* not fair, interfering in my life. Mind your own business. Leave us alone.'

What was the matter with me? I never knew I could be so cruel.

'Piss off!' she says.

'I'm going, don't worry.' I stumble to my feet, sending the Best Friend mug flying against the grate. There's a loud crack as it breaks in two. I grab my bag and coat and head for the door.

Outside a mist has come in but I hardly notice it as I run down the street, sobbing. Just who does she think she is?

At the end of the road I turn into a street of large semi-detached houses, set back from the pavement in gardens hidden by high, thick hedges. I come to a halt, my chest heaving, and scrub my wet face with my sleeve. Then I take a deep breath and swing my bag up on to my shoulder. Time to go home.

I set off down the long street, my heeled shoes echoing loudly in the silence. There is no one about and it's as black as pitch. A solitary car comes slowly towards me, its dipped lights bouncing back from the impenetrable murk. A cat streaks out of a garden and brings me to a halt with a squeal of fright.

I carry on walking again, my heart thudding. I don't feel safe in this dark, empty street with its high hedges and open gates where anyone could be lurking, waiting to pull you into their clutches. A tall bush looms in the driveway of a house. For a second I think it's a man and I freak out.

The road is longer than I thought, the end of it shrouded in fog. I feel disorientated and stop abruptly, wondering if I'm going the wrong way. I turn around to get my bearings, and out of the corner of my eye I think I can see a shadowy figure, but I blink and it's gone.

I peer into the gloom, rigid with fear. Don't be silly, there is no one there, it's your imagination playing tricks on you. But my heart is beating so fast it feels as if it is going to burst right through my chest. I turn around again and continue walking down the road, faster this time, my heels ringing out a desolate tune in the darkness.

And then I hear it. Quiet, but unmistakable. A soft, insidious undertone beneath the regular rhythm of my loud, clacky heels.

I stop and it stops.

I start and it starts too.

I quicken my pace and it speeds up.

Someone is following me.

I whiz around, my heart in my mouth, and I spot him, some way behind me. He stops but it's too late. I've seen him.

I shriek and now I am running as fast as I can down the pitch-dark street. He is chasing me. He's not trying to be quiet now. He's after me.

I can feel him gaining on me, closer and closer. I can hear his breathing, loud and rasping. I can sense him reaching for me, lunging forward . . . and I scream, as loud as I can, for the one person I know who would help me . . .

'JEEEEEEEEEEEEEEEEEEEMMMMMMMM!!!!!!!!'

Chapter 25

'Anna! It's OK. Anna! I've got you. You're all right.'

I peer up at him, afraid to look, and I can't believe my eyes. It's him. It's really him.

How could I do this? How could I conjure Jem up like this just when I needed him?

My knees sag and I sink to the ground, weak with relief. Jem crouches beside me, holding me safe in his arms.

'Someone was chasing me,' I sob. 'Where did he go? What happened to him?'

'It was me,' he says. 'I was following you.'

'What?' I look up at him. 'Why?' My voice rises in a shriek and then I'm hitting him on the chest, pummelling him as hard as I can. 'You scared me half to death, you stupid jerk. I thought you were after me!'

'I was.' He grabs my fists. 'Shhh. It's OK. I was trying to catch up with you.'

'Why didn't you say anything?'

'I didn't want to scare you. I'd been waiting for you for ages. But when you came out of Zoe's, you ran straight off. So I followed you to check you were OK.'

'What were you doing hanging outside in the dark?'

'I had to see you. You wouldn't answer your phone. You're right, I am a stupid jerk.' His voice breaks. 'I love you, Anna. I couldn't bear to lose you.'

He looks so contrite. I reach up to cup his cheek and he grabs my hand and presses it to his lips.

'You're not going to lose me,' I say. 'Ever.'

'Promise?'

'I promise. It was a row, that's all. Our first one.'

'And our last. I will never, ever let you get rid of me.'

We walk through the empty streets together, arms wrapped round each other. The night isn't scary any more, just peaceful. When Jem is on your side, there is no reason to be frightened of the dark.

When we get to Wharfside, I press the code and the front door swings open. As the lift whisks us up to the top floor, I am aware of Jem like I have never been before. Outside Dad's flat I hand him the key. When he opens the door, he carries me over the threshold and places me on the kingsize bed, the one my father shares with Jude. I can't help it, I freeze.

'No,' I say. 'Not here. It's not right.'

Jem looks down at me with amusement.

'I'm not going to make you do anything you don't want to do,' he says and I relax. My hand reaches up to the back of his head and I draw him back down to me, feeling his body against mine. Jem pulls away groaning.

'Shit, Anna, make your mind up. Don't mess me about.'

'It's OK,' I say. 'Don't stop.' And I forget all about what's right and wrong and lose myself in him.

When I wake up, Jem is sleeping, one arm flung up behind his head, the other curled around me. I feel incredibly peaceful. Until I turn my head, that is, and the clock radio tells me it is 00:09. I sit bolt upright with a gasp.

'What is it?' Jem struggles up on to his elbow.

'It's tomorrow!'

'So? We're staying here for the night, remember?'

'But I haven't told Mum! I forgot to go home first.'

'Tell her now.'

'You're joking!' I mean, I know my mum loves Jem, but even she's not that open-minded. 'She'll be worried sick.'

'She'd have rung you if she was bothered.'

'I switched my phone off, remember!' I grab it from my bag and switch it back on.

'What are you doing?'

'Ringing her. Telling her I'm on my way home.'

'Don't go.' Jem's hand comes over mine.

'I've got to!'

'No, listen. She thinks you're at Zoe's, right?'

'Right.'

'Then tell her you're staying the night.' His eyes are large, pleading. 'Please, Anna? Stay with me.'

'I'll try. But she might have spoken to Zoe already . . .'

Mum's not very happy when I get hold of her.

'Anna? Where have you been? I've been trying to get hold of you! I was just about to ring Zoe to find out where you were.'

'I'm sorry! We forgot the time. Been busy with revision, so I switched my phone off. Look, Mum, I might as well sleep over at Zoe's tonight, yeah?'

Mum hesitates. 'I suppose so.'

'I'll see you tomorrow after college.'

Mum sighs. 'OK. But let me know a bit earlier next time. I was starting to get worried!'

'Nah! You don't have to worry about me. I'm the good girl, remember?' But there's silence on the other end so I add lamely, 'Sleep well. Love you!' and click off.

'OK?' asks Jem and reaches out an arm to me. I snuggle in beside him, my head on his chest.

'Fine,' I say, and he kisses the top of my head, and within minutes I can tell from his regular breathing, he's fast asleep again. But even though I am spending the night wrapped in the arms of the man of my dreams, in a kingsize luxury bed, I lie there wide awake in the darkness, my head in a whirl.

Chapter 26

Jem wakes me in the morning with breakfast on a tray complete with pink carnation in a vase. I peer at it in amazement. There's cereal, bacon and eggs, toast and marmalade, and a glass of what looks like sparkling orange juice with a strawberry and a slice of orange in it. I take a sip.

'Wow! This is gorgeous.'

'It's Buck's Fizz. Champagne and orange juice.'

'Champagne?'

'You know, the fizzy stuff.' His eyes are alight with laughter.

'I know what it is, idiot. Where did you get it?'

'I found a case of it in the cupboard. Don't worry, he won't miss one.'

'Jem! Of course he will! You'll have to replace it! And the bacon and eggs and stuff!'

'I will. Now shut up and enjoy your breakfast.'

I sit back against the pillows and take another sip. 'I could get used to this.'

'You can. For the next few nights, anyway.'

'You reckon?' I poke my toast into the egg and take a bite. 'Delicious. How did you know this is the way I like my eggs?'

'Oh, I know everything about you.' Jem grins and tops up my glass with more champagne. 'Nothing escapes me.'

I grin at him happily as the yolk runs down my chin. 'Do you know, I'm beginning to think you do!'

I'd love to stay in bed with Jem all day but, mindful of my meeting with Mrs Hopkins, I tear myself away and jump into the shower. She's nice, Mrs H, she's on my side. I'm kind of looking forward to a friendly chat with someone since my big-time falling-out with my best mate last night.

When I come out of the shower, he's reading in bed.

'What's the book?'

He shows me the cover. It's a diary. Jude's.

'That's private!'

Jem grins. 'That's why it makes interesting reading! Wanna look?'

For a second I'm tempted. Then I say, 'Nah, I'm late,' and I busy myself getting dressed.

When I kiss him goodbye, he tries to pull me back into bed, but I resist.

'When will you be back?' he moans.

'As soon as I can,' I laugh, managing to wriggle out of his arms.

By the time I make it into college, I've missed first period, but I'm waiting for Mrs H outside her office when she bustles along at break-time. I could swear for a second she looks relieved when she catches sight of me, but she just gives me a tight little smile and ushers me inside with the words, 'Take a seat. I'll be with you in a second.' Then she totally ignores me, clicking on her computer instead and staring at the screen, her face expressionless.

I might look composed but inside I'm a bundle of jangling nerves. I've left Jem in the apartment and, though I don't like to admit it to myself, that worries me a bit. I'm not sure why – I trust him, don't I? I mean, he's hardly going to go through my father's bank accounts or steal the family jewels, is he? And anyway, who am I to talk?

I'm sitting here in my tutor's office wearing a pair of Jude's knickers. A black, lacy thong! Jem's choice. I had no clean underwear so he went through her drawers and found it for me. He doesn't seem to get the privacy thing

– he thinks it's hilarious, but it really freaks me out. Plus, despite my sobering power-shower, I'm feeling slightly drunk after my champagne breakfast. It's all kind of surreal.

Mrs Hopkins clicks her screen shut purposefully and swings around to face me.

'Anna? Have you got anything you want to tell me?'

'What?' Her words wrong-foot me. What does she mean?

She takes a deep breath. 'Where were you this morning?'

'Pardon?' I stare at her blankly. I'd nearly broken my neck getting here on time for this meeting. I didn't have to do this. I could still be fast asleep in Jem's arms. She was the one who wanted a cosy little chat, not me.

'First lesson?' she prompts.

'I was here,' I lie.

'That's strange. I didn't see you in English.'

My blood runs cold. I'd forgotten it was English first thing. Her lesson.

'I had a dental appointment.'

'Really?' She turns back to the computer and opens up the screen again, turning it towards me so I can see it too. It's a record of my attendance. Or rather, of my absences. 'And did you have a dental appointment last Friday, period two? Or Thursday afternoon? Or all day Wednesday?

Or the week before when you missed double Sociology, three periods of Art and an important lecture by a guest speaker on Flaubert?'

Her voice is different this morning. Accusatory. 'I've been doing a little research, Anna. I can see that recently you've been missing a large number of sessions. Can you explain why?'

'I've been trying to catch up.' I mumble.

'The more lessons you miss, the more difficult it will be to catch up.'

'I know that!' I rub my brow, between my eyebrows where a headache is building up momentum. I can feel her gaze on me.

'Did you go home last night?'

My head jerks up in surprise. 'Yes!' Only I can feel my face burning and I can tell she doesn't believe me. How does she know, the witch?

'You're dressed in the same clothes as yesterday,' she says, as if she's read my mind. 'In all the time I've known you, you've never done that before.'

'Yeah, well, there's always a first time!' I say. Just who does she think she is? 'I don't comment on the clothes you wear!' I add.

'You're not paid to keep an eye on me,' she says crisply. 'On the other hand, I am paid to look after your welfare

179

here at college as well as teach you English. It's my job. It's important to me that you do well, Anna, that you make the most out of your time here, get good grades . . .'

'Yeah, you wouldn't want me to fail my exams, would you? That would really mess up your league tables!'

She has the grace to look embarrassed. 'Yes, it would,' she admits. 'It would look even worse if you dropped out altogether.'

Dropped out? Who said anything about dropping out? Suddenly I feel scared. She's not going to give me the push, is she?

'You're a clever girl, Anna. One of the best I've ever taught. But you've got to put the work in if you've got your sights set on an English degree at a decent university.'

'I've changed my mind. I think I'll do Art instead.'

'Really?' She stares at me in surprise. 'Mr Thomas tells me you rarely bother to turn up there, either.'

I stare at the floor.

'Anna.' Her voice is gentle now and, paradoxically, this makes me want to cry. 'Don't do this. Don't throw away all your opportunities for some boy . . .'

Some boy? How does she know so much about me? I stare at her, open-mouthed while the penny drops. 'Huh! I get it. You've been talking to Zoe, haven't you?'

'She was worried about you when you didn't turn up at college this morning.'

'Yeah, right!' I burst out bitterly. 'She chucked me out in the middle of the night!'

Slight exaggeration, but Mrs Hopkins nods understandingly. 'Zoe explained that you'd had a row and had left her house, upset. She was very concerned when there was no sign of you in English, and confided in me. Nobody else knows, though I was just about to contact your mother to see if you'd got home safely.'

I swallow, grateful at least that my presence here this morning had scuppered that little idea. Mum, for all she liked him, would've had a fit if she'd known I'd lied to her and spent the night with Jem. Especially in Dad and Jude's bed!

And I can't even begin to think what *they* would say if they knew about it!

Suddenly it all feels a bit mucky. Tacky. Sordid. Though at least I'd got away with it and no one ever need know.

But then Mrs Hopkins says, 'Maybe it would be a good idea to ask your parents to come in to see me anyway? We could have a chat about your progress, set up a programme to get you back on track before it's too late . . .'

'NO!' The last thing I needed was for my parents to be

informed about how rubbish I was and what a bad influence Jem was on me. 'It's difficult at the moment at home. My parents have split up. Dad's . . . not here . . . he's in New York . . . working. And my mum's not very well at the moment. It would only worry her.'

'Oh.' The teacher's face droops with concern. 'I'm sorry to hear that. That does explain a lot. But I do feel they need to be kept in the picture, before it's too late . . .'

'Look, I'm fine, really. OK, I know I've been slacking a bit lately, but I'm back on track, honest. Now I've dropped Sociology, I can concentrate on the others and prepare properly for my A levels. Maybe you could give me a hand with English, help me catch up . . . ?'

Mrs Hopkins smiles. 'Of course I will,' she says and dives into her filing cabinet. Five minutes later, I stagger from her office with a stack of notes and past papers a mile high.

That's my trouble. I'm too good an actress.

Outside, Zoe is waiting for me, hopping anxiously from one foot to the other, arms folded tight with tension.

'Anna! Are you OK? I was so worried!'

'Yeah, right. For your information I got chased by some nutter. I could've been attacked and left for dead for all you cared!'

Why did I say that? It was Jem – I was in no danger whatsoever. Maybe because at the time, before I knew it was him, I had been truly terrified. It has the desired effect anyway. Zoe's face is blank with shock.

'Oh my G—'

'Yeah, thanks a bunch!' I say, glaring at her over my pile of papers. 'And not only did you chuck me out of your house last night, you and your big mouth nearly got me chucked out of college!'

She stares at me in horror. 'I'm so sorry! I was worried sick about you when you didn't turn up this morning. And Mrs Hopkins asked where you were and I couldn't help it, I—'

'I know, she told me.'

'I'm sorry!' she repeats miserably. 'It's all my fault.'

'Some friend you turned out to be!'

'Anna, if there's anything I can do to make up . . . Anything?'

'Yes there is. Stay away from me!'

I stalk off down the corridor, enjoying the sight of her mortified face. It makes me feel better somehow.

I can't think about my own role in all this. Not yet.

I've got other things to do.

Chapter 27

It's my last chance.

So what? It doesn't matter, does it? I'm going to London with Jem whether I pass my A levels or not.

In the library I sink down into a chair and put my head in my hands. It does matter. It matters a lot. Not for Mrs Hopkins' sake, not for Zoe's, certainly not for my father's, not even for my mum's.

It matters to me.

I want to be a student. I realize that now. I want to for all the obvious reasons, but also because I actually *like* studying. It's what I'm good at. It's just that since I've met Jem, life has become such a whirl I haven't found time to do it.

But it's not too late. I take a deep breath and start ploughing my way through the notes.

I keep my phone switched off and scribble away madly,

trying to catch up on weeks of work. I hadn't realized how much I'd missed. Soon I am totally absorbed, not even noticing it's lunchtime till Zoe drops in front of me a tuna and cucumber sandwich (my favourite) from the canteen. I ignore her, but eat it later on my way to afternoon lessons.

In French I keep my head down and collect extra work at the end from Madame Cassian, who's obviously already been briefed by Mrs H. We've got a test tomorrow and I'm way behind with revision. In Art I refuse to rise to sarcastic observations from Mr Thomas about my attendance or the lack of it and just get down to it.

By the end of the day I'm exhausted, but satisfied. I can do this, I know I can. Zoe is waiting for me outside the Art room.

'How did it go?' she asks quietly.

'Good.'

'I'm glad!' She grins, delighted she's got a response. 'I'll help you as much as I can, you know that!' She puts her arm through mine, but I shake it off. The thing is, I'm not mad at her any more. None of the mess I've got myself into is her fault, but I'm not quite ready to let her off the hook yet. I stare at her, unsmiling.

'If we're going to stay friends, you have to get over this thing you've got about Jem,' I say.

'I haven't got a thing about him!' she starts to protest, but I interrupt her.

'Yes you have. You don't like him, Zoe, I'm not stupid. But he's my boyfriend and I love him. It's serious between us. So if you can't accept that, well . . .' I shrug my shoulders.

She bites her lip. Zoe knows me better than anyone. She knows that if I had to choose between them, I would choose him.

'OK. I'll be honest with you, Anna, I'm no fan of Jem's. No, listen!' she says urgently, as I turn away in a huff. 'I am a fan of yours though, so I'll try, for your sake. He must be all right if you like him that much. OK?'

'Thanks.' I give her a squeeze. 'Once you get to know him properly, you'll love him too, I promise.' She doesn't look convinced so I add, 'Well, you'll like him. A bit? A teeny bit?' My voice is high and wheedling, and I'm rewarded at last with a reluctant smile and an 'Idiot!'

'Go on!' I say, 'Admit it! He's hot.'

'Oh yeah, he's hot all right!' she concedes a bit grimly, but I let it pass. It's a start.

I slip my arm through hers and we walk out of college together, buddies again. Across the road I spot Jem waiting for me. As he walks towards me I warn Zoe, 'Now be nice!' and she says, 'I will!' and fixes a smile on her face.

187

But it's Jem who's not nice.

'Where the hell have you been?' he says, glowering at me.

'College,' I say in surprise.

He completely ignores Zoe gawping at him as he confirms her worst prejudices. 'You said you weren't going to be long. I've been waiting round for you all day.'

'I had lectures to go to!'

'You could've rung me!'

'Sorry,' I say, remembering that my phone was turned off. I am so aware of Zoe taking all this in as I attempt to explain. 'I got hauled over the coals. They were on the point of chucking me out.'

'So?'

Is he doing this deliberately? 'Well, I had to get some work done, didn't I?'

He scowls even more. 'Why? I thought we'd decided you're not going to sit your A levels anyway.'

Beside me I hear Zoe gasp.

'*We* haven't decided anything!' I say in a flash of annoyance and our eyes lock together defiantly.

'Look, I'd better go,' says Zoe and she dashes off.

Jem mutters something after her. I don't quite catch it but I can tell it's not very nice.

'Don't take it out on her!' I snap.

'Why not?' he snarls. 'She's the one who's turned you against me. Bitch!'

We're like two dogs circling each other, ready to go for each other's throat. Suddenly I can't stand it any more.

'Stop it! Stop it, Jem!' I yell. 'Why do you do this? Why do you think everyone is against you all the time?' But I know the answer to this already. He doesn't trust people, especially women. No wonder, with a past like his. 'Zoe hasn't turned me against you.'

'She wants to split us up!'

'She doesn't, she wants to be friends. She's not the enemy, Jem. She's on our side.'

He looks sceptical but says nothing. I can tell he doesn't believe me, but at least he's calmer. He gazes into the distance for a while, his arms folded tight across his chest, then all of a sudden he groans. 'I'm sorry, Anna. You're right. I just missed you so much. Last night was amazing.'

His eyes are so warm and full of regret they melt all my anger away and I put my arms around him.

'For me too. Don't let's quarrel.'

I can feel his lips against my hair, his hands smoothing it down. 'I love you,' he murmurs. 'Come back to your dad's flat.'

'I can't. I've got to go home. Mum will be worried.'

'Tell her you're staying at Zoe's again. For the next few days. Catching up with work.' His voice in my ear is low and insistent. 'It's true, you can get it done, I won't disturb you. And then, when you've finished it all, we can spend the night together.'

'I can't . . .'

At this moment there is nothing I want more.

'Please . . . Zoe will cover for us. You said she wants to be friends.' I can feel his body against mine.

'I'll have to go home first and tell Mum . . .'

'Ring her.'

'I need to collect some stuff . . .'

'There's stuff in the flat.'

'I can't, I mustn't . . .'

He takes my hand in his.

'Anna,' he says, 'you're coming with me.'

He hadn't expected this. This wasn't part of the plan.

But that's the way it always happened.

Love crept up on you like a thief in the night and Bang! Bang! Got you right through the heart.

But love left you confused.

And defenceless.

Chapter 28

Things don't work out exactly as planned. We go back to the flat and fall straight into bed. Afterwards, I lie in Jem's arms, listening to the steady beat of his heart, and it strikes me how rapidly our relationship has developed and changed. Not very long ago it was easy, fun, uncomplicated. Now it's intense, fiery, fuelled by rows and misunderstandings.

And fear.

Fear? Where did that come from? Lying there with my head on his chest, I feel my forehead crease into a frown. Am I afraid of Jem? I rise up on my elbow to look at him sleeping peacefully beside me. His face is softer in sleep somehow, like a child's. Of course I'm not afraid of him.

I study him, drinking him in. I love the way his hair grows, thick over his brow; I love his long, dark lashes; I love his jaw, relaxed now in sleep but still firm and almost blue with its barely controlled stubble; I love his straight nose and his olive skin and the smell of him and the glimpse of white, slightly crooked teeth between his lips . . .

It's his mouth I love most of all, his beautiful mouth. I love the clearly defined but asymmetric lips with the barely discernable lift at one side that hints of darker depths. I could die for that mouth . . .

He opens his eyes and smiles up at me, sleepily. I dip my head and press my lips to his and he pulls me back down into the haven of his arms.

I love him.

Chapter 29

My phone wakes us up. It's Mum, wanting to know if I'm coming home for dinner. I struggle up on to my elbows.

'I'm at Zoe's, Mum. We're revising for our French test tomorrow.' Jem nudges me and I add, 'I think I might stay over.'

'*Again?*'

Mum's voice is suspicious.

'We've got loads to do. It's easier, working together.'

There's silence on the other end. Then Mum says, 'You're not with Jem, are you?'

'No! Of course I'm not with Jem!' Jem grins and starts to tickle my leg. I brush his hand away impatiently.

'Only it's strange how we haven't seen hide nor hair of him since you've been at Zoe's.'

'He's working, Mum. That's why I'm taking the

opportunity to catch up. You don't want me to fall behind, do you?'

'No, of course not.' Mum's voice is still uncertain. 'So long as Zoe's mother doesn't mind. Can you put her on? I'd like a word with her.'

'She's out.'

'Zoe, then?'

'She's in the shower.'

'Anna? What are you up to?'

'Mum! Trust me!' I say, and end the call. Then I put my face in my hands and groan.

'Maybe I should just get dressed and go.'

'No! Don't be daft! You've got work to do. By the time you get home, it'll be too late to do anything. Look, I'll make you a nice meal while you get on with it.'

'But what about Mum? She doesn't believe me, I can tell. She wants to speak to Zoe.'

'Then ring her! Get her to phone your mum and tell her you're there with her.'

'I can't ask her to do that!'

'Why not? You said she was on our side.'

I sigh and call Zoe.

'You OK?' she asks.

'Yeah, I'm fine,' I say, puzzled, then remember she'd left at the point Jem was being a brat. 'I'm at—' Just in time I remember to stop myself blurting out that I'm squatting in my dad's apartment with my boyfriend. I don't think Zoe would understand. 'Look, Zoe, I'm going to stay at Jem's for a night or two.'

'I thought he shared a room with two other blokes?'

'He does. But they're away.'

'Well, that's up to you, if that's what you want to do. What are you telling me for?' She sounds a bit cheesed off. Nothing new there.

'The thing is, Zo, I've told my mum I'm staying with you. To revise for French.'

'So?'

'I'm not sure she believes me. Can you ring her?'

'You want *me* to ring *her*? What for?'

'So she knows it's true.'

'It's not true.'

Silence.

'You want me to lie for you, tell her you're at my house.'

'Yeah.'

'You're kidding.'

'Please, Zoe.'

'And what am I supposed to say if she wants to speak to you?'

'Tell her I'm busy. Tell her I'm on the loo! Make

197

something up! Please, Zoe. For us.'

My voice is pleading. There's silence on the end of the line. Then finally she says, 'For *you*.'

A message comes through from Zoe five minutes later. It's short and to the point. *Sorted*, it says. Not even an 'x', let alone a 'lol'. But by that time I'm deep into my French revision, books scattered all over the bed and a glass of fizz in my hand, while Jem potters around in the kitchen getting some food together. It feels ace, like we're a proper couple. If this is a sign of things to come, then I can't wait to live with Jem in London. Bring it on!

That night we eat olives, sun-dried tomatoes, peppers, anchovies and little biscotti things that Jem has found in the cupboards. Very Mediterranean. And we drink champagne, of course. Afterwards he produces a box of dark chocolates, laced with brandy, which are totally delicious.

'I'll be pissed!' I moan as I help myself to yet another. 'And I've still got loads of work to do.'

'No problem,' he says, topping up my glass. 'I'm going to disappear for a while, let you get on with it.'

'Are you going out tagging?' I say in surprise.

'Nope. I'm going round to yours. Allay your mum's suspicions. Then she'll think you really are at Zoe's.'

'That is so clever!' I say admiringly. 'When will you be back?'

'I won't be long.' He plants a kiss on the top of my head. 'Now, get on with it! Leave the washing up. I'll do it when I get home.'

Home. He'll do it when he gets home. That is so sweet. I stretch out in the bed as he shuts the door behind him. I wish it was our home.

I wish I really lived here with Jem.

He lengthened his stride comfortably, feeling his heart rate increase. It was good to keep fit, to stretch out. He spent too much of his time hanging around, keeping an eye on things. He got worked up that way.

Now, running alone through the streets, he felt better. Calmer. More in control.

Was this what happiness felt like?

Chapter 30

I'm fast asleep when Jem returns. I'd worked on my French for hours till my eyes drooped and my brain refused to cram in any more. I can't actually remember falling asleep, but the next morning I wake up with a thumping head.

Jem is sprawled out beside me, snoring gently. I kick him grumpily and he opens his eyes.

'What time did you come in last night?'

'Dunno. Not that late. You were flat out so I didn't disturb you.' He reaches out for me but I shake my head.

'I've got a splitting headache.'

He laughs and says, 'You're supposed to use that excuse when we're old and married.'

'It's true!'

He leans across and picks up the empty bottle of champagne on my side of the bed. 'I'm not surprised. You finished this off last night when I was out.'

'Did I?' I remember now. I was sipping it all the time I was revising. Champagne is weird; you don't feel as if you're drinking. Until the hangover kicks in.

'I've got my test this morning,' I say glumly.

'You'll be fine,' says Jem and he turns over and snuggles back down under the covers. 'Make us a cup of tea, babe, if you're getting up.'

By the time I bring it to him, he's gone back to sleep.

I struggle my way through the French test, hopefully doing enough to keep the teacher happy. In English I get a funny look from Mrs Hopkins when I first walk in, but I sit down and take off my sweater to reveal a top belonging to Jude and she visibly relaxes. She is so on my case, that woman!

I don't like wearing Jude's clothes, but beggars can't be choosers. I can't keep wearing the same clothes three days in a row; if Mrs Hopkins notices, you can bet everyone else does too.

Jem was snoring his head off when I left so I didn't get a chance to ask him how he'd got on at my house last night. Today I remembered he was working at lunchtime so I'd left him a note to say I'd see him back at the flat after college.

'How's the honeymoon going?' Zoe asks at lunchtime.

'Great.'

'You look knackered.'

I shrug and she looks away as if she's a bit embarrassed. I'm about to say, 'It's only a hangover!' but I think better of it. Instead I say, 'Thanks for covering for me with my mum. Was she OK about it?'

She nods. 'I told her you were staying with me for a few days. She believed me.'

'Thanks.'

'I don't like lying to your mum.'

'I know. I'm sorry. I won't ask you again.'

'Good. When are you going home?'

'Tomorrow.'

She finishes her sandwich and gets up from the table. I look up in surprise. 'Where you off to?'

'Library. Got some work to do.'

'OK. Thanks again, Zo.'

She hesitates, like she wants to say something else. I smile up at her, waiting.

'When's your dad back, by the way?' she says, finally.

'Tomorrow.'

'Thought so,' she says. 'Nice top.' Then she walks away.

I watch her go, the smile wiped clean from my face.

She knows.

I'm all over the place that afternoon. I need to speak to Zoe. I don't know what I'm going to say but I need to speak to her.

I want her to think it's OK to use Dad and Jude's flat while they're away, that they've given us permission to do so.

But I know she won't believe me.

I want to convince her, like Jem's convinced me, that it's no big deal.

But it is.

I want her to know I'm not a bad person.

We're in different lessons so at the end of the day I make sure I slip out of Art early and am waiting outside Psychology for her when the bell goes. But a crowd of them spill out together, laughing and talking, and she doesn't notice me standing there to the left, as she turns right and walks away down the corridor, chatting. I follow her as she leaves the building and makes her way across the car park, smiling, waving goodbye to people, all the time talking nineteen to the dozen to some girl from Psychology. I don't know her name. The two of them stroll off together down the road and not once does she turn around to see where her BFF is. Not once.

I make my way in the opposite direction, to Dad's

apartment. It's two bus journeys from college and by the time I get there I feel drained. I can't wait to see Jem.

But when I let myself into the flat it's dark and empty. The blinds are still drawn from the night before and there's no sign of Jem. No note. Nothing.

He must be still at work. I open the blinds. The flat looks worse in the half-light. Dirty plates, mugs, glasses and dishes from breakfast and last night litter the place. How can two people make that much mess? I heave a big sigh and pick up a bowl of half-eaten olives from the floor. Last night they were seductive. Today they are repellent.

I chuck them in the bin and walk into the bedroom. The bed is unmade and in the en-suite bathroom there are damp towels on the floor and tiny dark hairs in the sink. Jem has used my dad's razor, the expensive one Mum bought him for Christmas the year before last – he's left it on the side of the bath. Anger rises in my throat. He could've cleared up after himself, the lazy git, he could've cleared up the whole flat instead of leaving it for me to do. Where is he, anyway? I ring his number but his phone is turned off.

In the kitchen I switch the kettle on and start to pile things into the dishwasher. But when the kettle boils I give up and make a cup of tea, slumping down on to the sofa with it. I've got A levels coming up, I remind myself crossly. I've got work to do. Jem can do this lot when he comes home.

But Jem doesn't come home. I try to write up my History of Art homework but I find it hard to concentrate. I try his phone again but he's not answering. At eight o'clock I raid the fridge and make myself a bacon sandwich, but it sticks in my throat and I can't swallow. Where could he be?

I fight down the panic that is threatening to engulf me. I need to contact someone to find him, that's what I need to do. But when I pick up my phone I don't know who to ring. Not for the first time I realize how little I actually know about him. Something must have happened, but I have no way of finding out what.

Mum. She'll know what to do. But she thinks I'm with Zoe. And I can't ring Zoe and tell her I've lost Jem. Stop panicking, I tell myself, he's probably still at the hotel; maybe he was told to work on. Ring the hotel! That's the thing!

By the time I've phoned directory enquiries, got the number and managed to get through, it's gone ten o'clock. The bored receptionist finally informs me after keeping me on hold for ages that Jem Smith left work shortly after three p.m.

I sink back on to the sofa. I knew it! He must have had an accident. Should I ring the hospital? Should I report him missing? My hand reaches for my phone again.

Hold on. Call 999 and you'll have the police around here. Take a deep breath and calm down. Now, think! What's he likely to be doing at this time of night?

Tagging.

He could be with a girl, says a small voice.

Maybe he's left you.

Maybe he doesn't love you any more.

I try his number once more but it goes to answer phone.

So I ring the next number on my contacts.

I ring Livi.

Chapter 31

She answers straight away. I knew she would; her phone is a permanent extension of her right hand, like an extra digit.

'Hi, Anna!' she says breezily. 'How's the revision going?'

'Fine.' I take a deep breath, not sure of what I'm going to say, trying to keep the worry from my voice. 'Look, daft question, I know, but I don't suppose you've seen anything of Jem today, have you?'

'Duh! He's sitting here right next to me. D'you want him?'

I am stunned. I forget to answer. Then I hear Jem's voice on the line. 'Anna? You OK?'

'What are you doing there?' I ask in surprise.

'Came over after work, since you're at *Zoe's*,' he says, stressing her name warningly.

'I've been worried! Why didn't you let me know where you were?'

'Sorry. Your mum asked me to stay for dinner. I didn't realize the time.'

'Why didn't you answer your phone?'

'It didn't ring.' I can hear him fumbling about then he says, 'Oops! Forgot to switch it back on after work. Sorry!'

'It's all right, Anna!' shrieks Livi's voice in my ear. 'We've been looking after him!'

'Get off!' I can hear Jem laughing and Livi giggling, like he's trying to wrestle the phone from her. 'It's *my* phone!' she yells and there's more shrieks and laughter like they're fighting over it. She must have won because she comes back on.

'You can have him back!' she pants, out of breath. 'He eats too much anyway. Roast last night, curry tonight. He's eating us out of house and home!'

He must've snatched the phone off her again because there are more squeals, then I hear him say, 'I'm leaving this madhouse! I'll ring you!' and the phone goes dead.

I stare at it, bewildered.

Roast last night, curry tonight? There's me thinking we're having a secret few days together and Jem's been stuffing his face with my mother and sister for the past two nights. What the hell is going on?

I don't have long to find out. He rings me a few minutes

later, on his way home, all apologetic, but I refuse to listen. I stand at the window and watch as the bus draws up and he leaps off and runs across to Wharfside. When the buzzer goes I leave it, feeling a small surge of power as it goes again. But soon he is leaning on it and the continuous noise does my head in and I smack the button to let him in. He looks at me sheepishly as he peels off his jacket.

'Sorry.'

'I was worried! I didn't know where you were!'

'Sorry.'

'And all that time you were at my house with *my* sister and *my* mother filling your face with curry!'

'Sorry.'

'Stop saying that! I nearly called the police!'

He looks alarmed. 'You didn't, did you?'

'Of course not! What was I supposed to say? I've broken into this flat and now my boyfriend's disappeared! They'd think I was some kind of psycho or something!'

'You're not . . .'

'I know I'm not! But they'd think I was!' My voice rises alarmingly. 'And last night. We had a nice romantic meal together and then you left me, so I could get on with my work, you said, and you went round to my house and ate a *roast dinner*! What's going on, Jem?'

'Nothing! Look, sit down, Anna, you're all upset.'

'Too right, I'm upset.' But I allow him to take my hand and lead me to the sofa. And I allow him to keep my hand in his as he explains.

'I went round last night to give you a chance to get on with your work, yeah?'

I nod.

'Your mum had made a roast and she offered some to me. I said no, but she insisted!'

I sniff. I know what he means. My mother doesn't take no for an answer when it comes to food.

'Why didn't you tell me?'

'Because you were fast asleep when I got home, that's why.' He refrains from saying I was crashed out, drunk. 'Then this morning you were gone before I could say anything.'

I consider what he's saying. It all makes sense. But I'm not quite ready to let him off the hook yet.

'Still, you didn't have to do the same thing all over again tonight,' I say sulkily.

'Don't go moody on me, Anna. I didn't mean to. I only went around after work because I'm bored out of my mind without you.' He takes my hand and draws me into his arms. 'Anyway, think about it,' he says. 'It's a great alibi. It shows your mum that, obviously, we're not together.

214

You're revising at Zoe's, I'm at a loose end. She was pleased to see me and so was Livi . . .'

'I bet she was!' I mutter to myself. Livi worships the ground he walks on.

'Your mum sort of assumed I was staying for dinner again and it would've been a bit rude to leave straight after. Anyway, I thought it would give you time to get on with your work with me out of your hair for a bit.' He looks repentant. 'I've cocked up, haven't I?'

Jem is irresistible when he's sad. He's got that dark, soulful look that lends itself to misery.

'Come here,' I say, my anger all spent, and his face lights up. We kiss and make up and then he stretches out on the sofa, his head in my lap.

'I don't deserve you,' he says.

I trace the outline of his lips with my finger, wondering how I can hate him so much one minute and love him so much the next. It's not his fault – it's me, I'm all over the place. I mean, what was going on in my head? My boyfriend goes out of his way to allow me to get on with my work, spending two boring evenings with my mother and my kid sister for my sake, and what do I do? Freak out! Make out he's some kind of lying criminal.

'It's me that doesn't deserve you,' I confess. 'I was so

mad at you, Jem, when I came home. I was dying to see you and you weren't here . . .'

'I'm here now,' he says, kissing the tips of my fingers.

'. . . And the flat was in a mess, and I was horrible. I wouldn't clean it up on my own . . .'

'We can do it together in the morning.' He reaches up and pulls me down towards him. 'We've got more important things to be getting on with now.'

Chapter 32

I wake up, needing the loo, and check the time on the clock. Not yet six a.m. Quietly, I slip from between the sheets, trying not to disturb Jem. Afterwards I get a glass of water and wander over to the bedroom window to drink it. It's still dark outside and so silent I think I can almost make out the melodic clinking of the boats in the harbour. No one is around yet.

But then as I peer down at the empty Wharfside, my forehead resting against the cool glass, a taxi draws up. I can just see the top of it from where I'm standing. Late-night clubbers, I think. Young professionals from the apartments on their way home.

The door opens, the one furthest away from the kerb, and a girl gets out. I gasp aloud. Even from this angle, I can tell it is Jude. In horror I crane to see if my father appears out of the nearside door. I catch a brief glimpse of the top of his head and jump back in a panic.

'Jem!' I scream. 'Wake up! My dad's home!'

'What?' He sits bolt upright, his face almost comical with sleepy confusion.

'Dad! And Jude! They're here!'

His expression clears and he jumps to his feet and peers down into the road. The taxi driver has got out now and he and Dad have moved round to the boot.

'Shit!' he says and pulls on his jeans. Frantically, I start to snatch my clothes up from the floor where I had discarded them the night before.

'Where's my bra?' I say desperately. 'I can't find my bra!'

'Here it is!' Jem thrusts it into my hand. I fasten it with shaking hands and pull my sweater over it. Then I drag on my jeans.

'My sock, I've lost a sock. Put the light on!'

'No!' hisses Jem, hopping about madly, trying to stuff his foot into his shoe. 'They'll see us. Put your shoes on and grab your stuff, they'll be here in a minute.'

'My books!' I run into the lounge and scoop everything up from the floor where all my college work is strewn, stuffing it into my bag.

'Quick!' orders Jem, standing guard by the window. 'Shoes! He's paying the driver.'

I force my feet obediently into my boots. 'My make-up!' I run over to the dressing table and sweep some into my bag though it's hard to tell in the dark what's mine and what's Jude's. 'I've left stuff in the bathroom!' I cry, making a dash for it. Jem grabs me by the hand as I pass him, bringing me to a halt.

'No!' he shouts. 'Leave it! There's no time!'

'But my wash-stuff . . . and my sock . . . !' I'm flapping now like a headless chicken, and he yells back, 'I'll buy you a bloody sock!' but that's not what I mean.

I peer round him to see my father bending down to pick up two heavy cases. Jude has an armful of shopping bags. She rubs the back of her neck as if she's tired from travelling, then stretches her neck backwards to look up towards the window. Immediately, Jem steps back, treading heavily on my foot.

'Ow!'

'Shit! She nearly saw me then! Come on!'

At the front door he shoves my coat into my hands and pushes me out into the corridor. Automatically I run to the lift and am about to press the button when Jem screeches, 'Stairs, idiot!' I look up to see that the indicator is glowing. Someone has pressed the button on the ground floor. Cold fear grips me as Jem grabs me by the hand and leads me to the stairs.

Together we race down five flights, our footsteps beating out a frantic, clattering rhythm that echoes back up through the otherwise silent building. I swear, as we reach ground level, I can hear the lift ping as it arrives at its destination on the top floor. Finally, we burst through the front doors into the cold desolation of the early morning. At the top of the road, the retreating lights of the taxi wink at us, then disappear from sight. Hand in hand, we tear off after it, down the empty street.

Chapter 33

I never, ever want to go through that again, as long as I live. When we'd got away, once he knew we were safe, Jem was fired up by it all, sparking with excitement. Like he was off his head on something. Like he'd been tagging. For him it was the same thing, he thrives on the thrill of the chase. But me, I was shit-scared, weak with fear and remorse, my conscience going into overdrive, filling me with horror at the thought of what we had done and how nearly we had been caught.

'No harm done!' scoffs Jem as he tucks into a bacon sarnie at the café we'd found open near the station. 'We borrowed some real estate lying empty for a few nights, that's all. Squatters' rights. Nothing wrong with that.'

For once his beautiful mouth makes me feel sick as I watch his strong teeth tearing into the food in hungry, feral bites. I couldn't eat a thing.

'Shush!' I glance round, scared someone will overhear us, but apart from the owner, who's glued to the TV, there's only an old guy, half asleep and stinking of alcohol, and a grossly fat woman in layers of filthy clothing who's muttering away to herself. 'We left it in a mess!' I whisper. 'We were going to clear up this morning, remember? Now they'll know someone's been there.'

'They'll know that all right,' he says and grins, before slurping his mug of tea. This morning, in this sleazy café, with greasy bacon fat on his chin, I don't know what I ever saw in him. He needs a shave and looks scruffy and unkempt.

I can talk. I need a shower and a complete change of clothes.

'I want to go home,' I announce.

'You can't,' he points out. 'Not till tonight, anyway. You're staying at Zoe's, remember?'

I nod, too wasted to talk. I'll have to go to college first. In yesterday's clothes.

Too late I remember the top I'm wearing is the one I wore yesterday. It belongs to Jude. So does my underwear.

'Oh no!' I groan aloud, covering my face with my hands.

'What's up?'

My blood chills as I recall I'd borrowed her knickers

222

the day before too. What was I thinking of? They'd still be there, in the apartment, together with my own discarded pair from the day before that. When I tell Jem, unbelievably he laughs out loud.

'So what? Worried they'll have your DNA on them? They're never going to be able to trace you through a pair of dirty knickers!'

'Don't be so gross!' I look at his mocking face and I want to slap it. Hard. 'You don't get it, do you?'

'What?'

I shake my head, speechless with shame. All I want to do is crawl into my bed, pull the duvet over my head and never get out again. I stand up abruptly. My chair clatters to the floor and the filthy old guy jumps out of his alcoholic stupor as I rush out of the door.

It's Art, first period. I'm the first one there. It wasn't even eight when I got to college. Breakfast was on in the canteen but I couldn't face it. Plus I don't want to see anyone, looking like this. So I sit on my own in the Art room for an hour, dizzy with tension and regret. By the time Bill Thomas walks in and comes to an abrupt halt, my head is thumping and I have a raging thirst.

'Tell me I'm dreaming!' he says, slapping his hand to his head. 'Anna Williams is here before me, raring to go.'

'Ha, ha!' I say drily, hoping against hope that he won't

perch in front of me with his legs splayed for a chin-wag but, of course, he does.

'How's it going, Anna?'

'Fine.'

He gives me the benefit of one of his intense looks over his specs and says, 'Hmmph!' as if he doesn't believe me. 'Get your homework done last night?'

'Yep.'

'Like me to take a look while it's nice and quiet?'

'If you want.'

I dig into my bag and manage to locate the History of Art homework among the stuff I'd crammed in there in the dark a few hours earlier. Mr Thomas takes the crumpled sheets and makes a play of smoothing them out and starts to read. After a while he says, 'Hmmph!' again and stares at me morosely.

'What?' Even to me, my voice sounds sulky.

'Not good enough, Anna.'

Shit. I lighten my tone. 'Give it to me straight, why don't you?'

But he's not playing. 'If I gave it to you straight, I'd suggest you go back and start A-level Art all over again. This is not worthy of you. Plus, I took a look at your portfolio yesterday. It's not up to much, is it? As far as I can see, it's just full of graffiti.'

I feel as if he's punched me in the stomach and I can't breathe. When I'd told my dad I'd chosen Art as one of my A-level subjects, he'd said, 'What for? Anyone can draw and splash paint on to paper.'

Wrong again, Dad. Wrong on so many counts.

I can't. I can't do anything right any more.

How did I get to this?

I stand up.

'Where are you going?'

I don't answer. I don't know.

'Anna, come back. We need to talk about this.' Mr Thomas sounds anxious now, but it's too late. As the bell goes and people start to pour into the Art room, I barge straight past them, shouldering my way through the door.

I didn't know I was holding my breath until suddenly I take two ugly, rasping gasps and tears start rolling down my cheeks. I hold on to the rail outside the Art block to stop myself falling blindly down the steps. People are looking at me but I don't care. A couple of girls stop and say, 'Anna, are you OK?' and I say, 'Yeah, I'm fine,' and they move off, whispering.

Soon the yard empties out as lectures start and I'm left on my own. I sink down on to the steps, and hug my knees to me, head bent, and give myself up to despair.

'Anna? What's happened?'

It's Ben. He crouches down beside me, pushing my hair away from my wet face.

'What's wrong?' he says and I turn into him. His arms go round me and I sob my heart out.

OK, she was upset now but she'd be fine when she'd calmed down. He loved her, he'd never stopped loving her, he never would.

He would be there for her.

Always.

Chapter 34

Someone tells Zoe that her best mate's having a breakdown on the steps of the Art block and soon she turns up and gets rid of Ben.

She's brilliant. She listens without interrupting as I gulp out my tearful tale of how I was nearly discovered by my own father in *his* bed with *my* boyfriend. Then she does something I don't expect.

She giggles!

'It's not funny!'

'It's hilarious! I can just imagine you two hopping around in the dark, trying to get dressed. It sounds like a farce!'

I sniff loudly. 'I suppose, when you put it like that. Then we had this mad race downstairs while Dad and Jude were coming up in the lift.'

She shakes her head, still spluttering. 'It would've

served you right if you'd got caught red-handed. I knew what you were up to, you know.'

'Do you think I'm terrible?'

'Nooo,' she says comfortingly. 'No harm done, is there? Who's to know?'

'That's what Jem says.' I feel better already.

'I was just mad at you because you didn't let me into your sordid little secret,' she confesses.

'Well, you know it all now.'

Not quite all. She doesn't know about the state we'd left the flat in, the food and drink we'd consumed, the clothes I'd worn. I pull my coat tighter around me. She's forgotten about Jude's top, the one she noticed yesterday, the one I'm still wearing right this minute. No need to remind her. No need at all.

'What was it like?' she asks suddenly.

'What was what like?'

'You know. Spending all that time with Jem. Together, in the flat. Just the two of you?'

Images from the past few days crowd into my mind:

A soft bed, the centre of our existence; damp towels on a bathroom floor.

Laughing and loving together; waiting and worrying, alone.

Falling asleep in each other's arms, drunk with love; waking up with a hangover.

Champagne and olives; morning breath and a raging thirst.

Jem's beautiful mouth; a borrowed razor, thick with hair . . .

'I'm sorry,' she says, her face pink. 'I shouldn't have asked.'

'No! It's just so hard to explain. It was . . . it was . . . *more.*'

'*More?* More what?'

'Just . . . more. More than anything else I've ever known.'

'Lucky!' she breathes.

But I'm not sure she's right. I don't know if I want *more.* I think I just want normal.

I muddle through the day somehow, keeping my coat on all the time, so Zoe and my eagle-eyed English teacher, Mrs H, won't notice the top I'm wearing. I bump into Mr Thomas again at lunchtime and he looks embarrassed and hummphs a bit and suggests that perhaps he (hummph, hummph) and I (hummph, hummph) overreacted and things aren't as bad as we

231

thought. Jem phones to see how I am, sounding really unfazed, and says he'll pop round this evening. It looks like life is returning to normal again, thank goodness.

At the end of the day, Zoe walks back to mine with me. Her suggestion, so Mum can see I've been staying with her. What a mate! Mum is already home and pleased to see us.

'Hi, girls! Productive few days? Get lots of revision done?'

'Not bad.'

'We've seen quite a lot of Jem since you've been at Zoe's. He popped round last night and the night before. I think he was missing you.'

'Yeah, he said. On the phone. He's coming round tonight too.'

'Thought he might be. He's one of the family now, you know.' Livi sidles round the door. I've only been away three days but she looks different somehow. Sort of cocky. She's changed out of her school uniform already and is plastered in make-up.

'Where you going?'

'Nowhere. Some of us care about the way we look,' she says, looking me up and down insolently. 'Is this the new grunge look you're cultivating?'

'Meow!' says Zoe and everyone laughs.

232

'Actually, I think I will go and grab a shower before dinner,' I say graciously, even though I'm aching to slap my sister's impertinent little face.

'No hot water at your house, Zoe?' asks Livi. I glare at her as I pass, then stop and sniff suspiciously.

'Is that my perfume you're wearing?'

'No!' she says, but her face goes pink.

'Better not be!' I say grimly. But upstairs I can tell she's been using it – the bottle's moved. Little thief!

Forget about it, Anna. You've just borrowed someone else's apartment without asking. Someone else's lifestyle. Don't begrudge your kid sister a drop of perfume.

I peel off my clothes, stuffing Jude's top and panties into the back of my wardrobe with a grimace, turn the shower up high and step in. The hot water makes me gasp, but I refuse to turn it down as it cascades over me, cleansing my body and my guilty conscience simultaneously in fierce, scalding blasts. Afterwards I dress from head to toe in clean clothes and dry my hair. As I sit with my head bent, hair dangling down in front of me, above the noise of the hairdryer I hear the doorbell and a deep, male voice downstairs. Jem's here already.

I stand in front of the full-length mirror, appraising myself. Clear brown eyes, thick straight hair, smaller than average but everything in the right place. I don't look any different from normal. Nothing to suggest I've spent the past three turbulent days, unbeknown to anyone but my best friend, in a secret love nest with my boyfriend.

I glance longingly at my bed, neatly made and inviting, my pyjamas, folded nicely, peeking out from under my pillow.

Later.

At the moment the man of your dreams is waiting downstairs for you, Anna. Most girls would give the world to be in your shoes.

I heave a huge sigh and go downstairs to see him.

Chapter 35

I push open the lounge door, expecting to see Jem, but it's my dad who's standing there in front of the fire. My mouth goes dry.

'What are you doing here?' I say.

'Anna!' says Mum. 'Your father's come to bring you a present from New York.'

'Look what I got!' says Livi and shows me an iPad. 'You've got one too.'

'Wow!' I take the shiny bag from his hand and peer inside. 'That's generous.'

'They're cheaper in the States,' says Dad. 'I was going to keep it for Christmas, but Jude said you'd need it for college.'

She would. I don't know what to say. 'Thanks.'

'That's all right.' Dad smiles at me and I smile back, nervously. This must have been one of the bags I'd seen

Jude clutching this morning.

As if she's reading my mind, my mum says, 'Your father had a bit of a shock when he arrived home this morning.'

Shut up, Mum, please. Just shut up.

I take the iPad out of the bag and make a show of examining it. 'This is amazing, Dad. Thank you.'

'Someone broke into his apartment while he was away!' declares Livi excitedly.

'Really?' I can't trust myself to look at Zoe. But then Livi asks, 'Did they take much, Dad?'

'Not a lot, as far as we can tell. My watch, some cash that was lying about, and a few personal items of Jude's, that's all.'

Zoe's jaw drops in surprise as I feel the blood draining from my cheeks.

'Your watch was stolen?'

'Yes, the one your grandma bought me when I qualified. That's the thing I'm mad about.'

'That was probably the most expensive gift she's ever bought anyone in her whole life,' says Mum softly. 'Don't tell her, she'll be upset.'

I think of my grandma, scrimping and saving to buy that expensive watch all those years ago for the high-achieving son she was so, so proud of, and I know I'm going to cry. It had to be Jem – there was no one else there, except me and him.

Zoe's voice, hard with anger, rings out. 'The bastard!'

'Yes,' agrees my mild-mannered mother. 'I think that's what we all feel, Zoe.'

'He took cash too?' asks Zoe.

'Yep. About two hundred and fifty quid, that's all. I don't leave much lying about.'

I feel sick.

'You mentioned a few personal items of Jude's?' prompts Mum.

'Bits of jewellery – gold mainly. He knew what he was looking for, all right. Left all the cheaper bits. And . . . he took some clothing, actually. A top she's particularly fond of.' He looks a bit embarrassed. 'And items of underwear.'

'Yuck!' says Livi, her little nose creased up in disgust. 'Pervert!'

'You said it!' says Zoe.

'Don't worry, sweetheart,' says Dad. 'I've had the locks changed. He won't be back.'

'What did the police have to say?' asks Mum.

'The police! You called the police?'

'Of course they did!' Livi looks at me as if I'm stupid. 'They got broken into, didn't they?'

Dad gives a little laugh. 'Actually, technically speaking, we didn't. There's no sign of a forced entry.'

'So how did he get in then?' asks Livi curiously. I stand there afraid to breathe. It's all going to come out now. It's pretty obvious.

I let him in.

'We must've left the door open when we left for New York. An open invitation to burglars.'

Silence falls. 'I find that hard to believe.' Mum voices what we're all thinking. Dad had an obsession for making sure our house was locked up every time we went out. Doors, windows, everything had to be secure. '*I come into contact with the dregs of society on a daily basis*,' he used to say when we complained.

He shrugs. 'I wasn't the last one out that morning,' he says and the unspoken feeling fills the room that this is all Jude's fault, only Dad is too loyal to say.

Except Zoe and I know what really happened. I can feel her eyeballing me, openly hostile. Suddenly, understanding floods through me, filling my veins with its toxic truth.

She thinks I had something to do with this.

'Anyway, there's loads of things he didn't take. Laptops, TV, Wii, iPods . . .'

'I wonder why?' says Mum.

'The police think he was more interested in using the flat than stealing stuff. That's the worst bit really. He'd been living in it while we were away, it's obvious. He left it in a right mess. We think he had a woman there as well.'

'How could you tell?' Zoe's voice is harsh.

'Some items that were left . . .'

My washbag. My pants!

Fortunately my father is discreet. 'It was obvious. They'd been eating our food, drinking our champagne, sleeping in our bed. He used my razor, she'd worn Jude's clothes. That's what freaks her out the most. She feels violated.'

'I'm not surprised!' Zoe growls in disgust. 'Some creep going through your stuff!'

I look at her in alarm. She won't say anything, will she?

Mum shivers. 'Where is Jude now?'

'Gone home to sleep at her parents' house. She says she never wants to set foot in the place again.' He looks gutted.

How ironic is that? All I ever wanted to hear was that he and Jude had separated. But I never meant it to happen this way. Even Mum looks sad.

'It's the shock,' she says gently. 'Give her time. She'll get over it.'

Dad smiles at her gratefully. 'The police think we surprised him, coming home when we did, and he had to make a quick getaway. They think he might have been watching us for a while, and took his opportunity when he saw us going off in a taxi with our cases. Probably thought we were away for a week or two.'

'Aahh!' Livi's sharp intake of breath makes us all turn to look at her. 'I've just remembered something. That time we stayed over at your flat, yeah? There was a bloke in the bus shelter opposite, watching us. Do you remember, Anna?'

'Yes.' Thank you, Livi, thank you, thank you, thank you, thank you for throwing them off the trail. 'Yes, I do. Then I noticed him again later that night, and he was still there, watching the flat.'

'You need to tell the police that, Dad. I bet it was him!' shrieks my sister in excitement and nobody but me notices that Zoe gives a snort of derision.

'I will. Did you get a good look at him?'

'Not really.' Livi's face clouds with disappointment.

'Don't worry. There'll be CCTV footage for them to look at.'

'CCTV?' I say, thunderstruck.

'Yes. They're studying it now.'

'Well, I hope they find him,' says Zoe venomously.

'Didn't the neighbours notice anything?' asks Mum.

Dad gives a wry laugh. 'You're joking. I wouldn't even know who my neighbours were.'

'Lucky you,' says Mum and they both laugh again. Even in my panic I can't help noticing that, weirdly, they're more relaxed in each other's company than they have been for months. And I wonder if, just maybe, some little bit of good will come out of all this mess.

Then the front doorbell rings and all hell lets loose.

Chapter 36

Livi jumps up, her face all bright and shiny. 'That'll be Jem!'

'Who's Jem?' asks Dad, just as I'm registering, how come she knows he's coming round?

'Anna's boyfriend,' explains Mum.

'I thought his name was James?' says Dad, bewildered, and my heart sinks. Then Zoe leaps to her feet.

'I'm going!' she announces angrily.

'I'll see you out!'

'Don't bother!' she snaps at me and rushes out of the door.

Mum and Dad stare at each other in surprise. 'What's up with her?' I hear Dad ask as I chase after her.

In the hallway, Zoe bangs straight into Jem.

'Whoa!' he says, laughing, and steps from one side to the other, his arms wide, blocking her way. 'What's the rush?'

'Piss off!' she snarls and pushes him in the chest so hard he staggers as she barges past him, straight out through the front door.

Livi's jaw drops open.

'Zoe, wait!' I shout.

'Leave me alone!'

'Zoe! I need to explain!'

'Let her go,' jeers Jem. 'She's nuts.'

Zoe comes to a halt and turns around, metres from the house, her face contorted with fury. She thrusts her arm out, pointing at Jem who is now standing beside me.

'And you are SCUM!' she yells and I hear Livi gasp.

Jem's lip curls and he saunters down the step towards her but she stands her ground. 'And YOU!' She turns her accusing finger towards me. 'You are the biggest loser I have ever met in my life.'

'What is wrong with her?' asks Livi, grabbing my arm.

'You involved me in all this, you bitch! You made me your alibi, and all the time you were scheming, planning . . .'

'Zoe! I didn't know—'

'Don't give me that! I believed you! I thought it was him! I thought he was the weird one! But you're just as bad . . .'

'What's going on out here?' Dad's strong hands grasp my shoulders and move me to one side and he stands at

244

the top of the step. 'What's all this about, Zoe?'

'Ask your freaking daughter!'

'Come inside and we can talk about it.'

'She's mad!' says Jem, a sneer on his face.

'I'm not mad, you are!' screams Zoe. 'And you!' She points at me again, beside herself with rage. 'You're twisted! You're worse than him . . . You'd screw over your own father to keep him happy . . .'

'Don't listen to her,' says Jem quickly. 'She's a psycho!'

'I'm not the psycho! You're the one who breaks into places. You're the one who steals. You're the one who trashes people's homes.'

'Oh God!' Behind me I hear Mum catch her breath.

Tears stream down my face.

'It wasn't like that!' I whisper as my legs give way and I stumble. An arm comes round my waist to support me. Dad's.

'Bitch!' Jem advances on Zoe, his face ugly with rage.

Mum brushes past me and wraps her in her arms and Zoe collapses against her, crying.

'How could you?' says Mum, metres from him. 'We trusted you! I trusted you with my daughter!'

Jem's face changes. It's open now, wide with affronted innocence. He spreads his hands wide, appealing to her. 'It's all lies,' he says. 'She's one mad cow! I've never even been inside your husband's flat.'

You can tell from her face she's nonplussed. She doesn't know what to think. Too late, I realize what a plausible liar Jem is.

But then Dad says, 'Who mentioned my flat?'

Silence.

Jem, realizing he's given the game away, lets out a small bark of derision. 'Is that what all this is about?' he says. 'Lighten up, man. We only stayed there a few nights.'

'Just go,' Dad says to him bleakly. 'Before I call the police.'

Jem's expression changes. It's crafty now, taunting.

'You know what, man?' Now it's his turn to point the finger, only he does it in a crude, one-fingered salute. 'You've got nothing on me. I didn't break into your flat. Your precious daughter invited me in!'

'Go now!' yells Dad. 'Before I change my mind. If I find you anywhere near my daughter again, I'll break your bloody neck!'

Jem backs away, cursing, then swaggers off down the road, yelling threats and expletives back at us.

Zoe throws her arms around me and my sobs turn to wails.

Someone else is crying too.

Livi is standing at the gate, watching Jem disappear, and the tears are streaming down her cheeks.

He always knew it would be her that came between them. Her and her big gob.

Fat cow. He could've carried this off it hadn't been for her.

Chapter 37

Jem has disappeared from my life as if he's never been there. At first he rings me twenty times a day and I tell him I never want to see him again.

I am so ashamed.

I remember when I told him Dad and Jude were going to New York. He was over the moon.

'*The answer to our prayers,*' he'd said. '*We can be together all night long.*'

And, stupid me, against my better judgement I'd allowed myself to be persuaded. I'd moved into my father's flat with him. I'd slept with him in my father's bed. I'd trusted him, leaving him on his own there – and this is how he'd repaid me. Helping himself to whatever he found lying about.

All I'd ever wanted from him was love. All he'd wanted from me was a free ride.

'You used me!' I say and he pleads with me, telling me it's all a big mistake, but I know he's lying. Then he turns nasty, saying horrible things about my family, especially Dad and Jude. (Since when did *she* become part of my family?) Most of it I'd said myself, but it sounds worse coming from him. He threatens to tell people I've been tagging with him all over town, but I tell him to get lost. He's done his worst. I know he won't do that anyway, he's got too much to lose.

I feel betrayed. Humiliated.

Then the phone calls, the texts, the Facebook messages stop and finally everything goes quiet. At last I can forget him.

But now, perversely, I can't get him out of my mind.

The truth is, I miss him.

Dad seems to be round a lot. He managed to coax Jude back from her parents, but I don't think she spends more time at the apartment than she has to. He says she doesn't feel safe there any more. She won't even look at the CCTV footage because she says everywhere she goes she'd be looking out for him if she knew what he looked like. You'd think she'd have a bit more bottle about her, with some of the clients she's had to deal with. Dad says that's the point, she's had trouble with one or two in the past.

'What sort of trouble?' asks Livi.

'Clients who think she's let them down because she didn't get them off.'

'What do they do?'

'Shout a bit when they get sent down. Make a few threats. It's happened to me countless times.'

'Scary!'

'No, it's all talk. They forget all about it once they're banged up inside. Interestingly, the one guy that really freaked Jude out was someone whose case she won. He wouldn't leave her alone after that, made out there was something special between them.'

'What happened?'

'I can't remember. It was a client from her last practice. She moved down here and he lost track of her, I guess.'

She moved down here and met you, we're all thinking.

Mum sighs. 'There are some strange people about, that's for sure. Take Jem, for instance. I really liked him.'

Here we go again!

'Yes, well, I blame myself for that,' says Dad.

'Why?' I say in surprise.

'I should've been there for you.'

'You were.' He warned me enough about Jem. I just wouldn't listen.

'I welcomed him into my home!' Mum says, looking stricken. 'He was always so pleasant, so well mannered . . .'

'Most psychopaths are!' says Dad bitterly.

'Jem's not a psychopath!'

'He stole my watch, my money and Jude's jewellery, let alone her . . . more personal items. Believe me, that's the hallmark of a nutter. I should know. I come across them every day!'

'Well, he said he didn't!' protests Livi. 'Why doesn't anyone believe him?'

'Because he's a flaming liar!'

I know Dad's right. To a point. He didn't take Jude's 'personal items'. Her pants and her top. That was me. But I'm too ashamed to admit it. The rest of the stuff though, he took that.

But no one can convince Livi. It's quite sweet really, the way she stands up for him, like a fox terrier defending a pit bull. As far as she's concerned, Jem can do no wrong. He's the injured party and there's a simple explanation.

'Jem's getting blamed for something he didn't do!' she maintains mutinously. 'Someone else could've broken into your apartment.'

'Don't be ridiculous,' says Dad.

'Well, maybe Jem had a mate around when Anna was at college and he helped himself.'

I sigh heavily. I'd thought of that too. But the truth was, Jem didn't have any mates.

'Leave it there, Livi.'

'Why don't you stand up for him?' she spits. 'You don't care about him! Nobody does!'

'I did care about him!' I snap back. 'I loved him! And look how he repaid me!'

'The CCTV footage shows there was no one else going in and out of the apartment except for Anna and Jem,' says Dad. 'It had to be him.'

'Or me!' I say venomously and Livi shuts up at last. But I know we haven't heard the last from her.

Dad didn't press charges. I know why. He didn't want to drag my name into it. With Jem out of my life, he hoped we could put the whole sorry incident behind us and move on with our lives.

But it's not as easy as that.

I try, I really do. I throw myself into college and spend all my time catching up. I can't believe how much I'd let things slide. Zoe's great. She's totally there for me now Jem's no longer on the scene. She helps me with my work, practically escorts me to and from college, and makes sure I hang out with her and the others in the common-room every lunchtime.

In a way, it's like Jem never existed. Secretly, I can't believe how easily he's given up on me. He said he loved me! I'd have thought he'd be more persistent than that.

I've seen him when he can't get what he wants and he never gives up. But now it's like my dream guy turned into a nightmare, and then I woke up and discovered he never existed at all!

Except I feel empty inside, like I've had something surgically removed. Jem has been aborted from my life and all that is left is a huge, gaping void of sadness and regret.

I can't sleep. Through the long, dark nights, I worry that I acted too hastily. Now I'm over the shock of what he did, I guess it wasn't *that* bad, after all. Maybe we all over-reacted. I mean, what did he actually do? Borrow my father's watch, drink his champagne (actually, I drank most of it!) and help himself to some money that was lying about, that's all. He probably intended to put it all back, but he didn't have time.

Let's face it, we'd left in a bit of a hurry that morning, which was the reason the flat was in such a mess. We didn't mean that to happen. OK, there was the matter of Jude's jewellery, but I can't remember seeing any lying about. Maybe she made it up? People do after a break-in, so they can claim on insurance.

And as for her clothing . . . well, that was me, not him, only I was too embarrassed to tell anyone. I let him take the rap for it, which did him no favours whatsoever.

Some girlfriend I turned out to be! He should've chosen Livi! She's never doubted him. Unlike me.

Loyal little Livi.

Jem, you chose the wrong sister. Livi would have stood by you.

Chapter 38

And then, just as I'm slowly coming to terms with the fact that Jem has vanished from my life for ever, he quietly lets me know he's still around. When I get to the bus stop one morning with Livi, I notice the shelter is boasting a JAWS tag inside a red heart. It looks just like the chocolate heart he slipped into my bag all those months ago – and I'm so taken by surprise, I gasp.

'What's up?' says Livi and I say, 'Nothing,' and she lapses back into the soulful silence that is becoming her default mood. Since Jem disappeared she's retreated into a world of her own – when she's not out with her giddy mates. I hope Ferret's not back on the scene now Jem's not here to set a good example. How ironic is that? That's something that Dad didn't see, the positive effect Jem had on my little sister. I think she misses him nearly as much as I do.

The next day there's a heart with a tag inside it on the pavement outside college. It's surrounded by a crowd of admiring students, who recognize the signature.

The day after that, one appears on the Art block.

Soon I'm looking for them – and he doesn't disappoint. One appears at the end of my street, another on our back door, a third on the wall of the corner shop. The message is loud and clear. Jem Smith is still around, Anna Williams, and he wants you to know he still loves you.

It's like *my* heart has lit up again. How did I think I could switch off what we had together? Every night, when I go to bed, I think of him out there, tagging. For me. Sometimes I think I'll go mad, I miss him so much.

One night I go to the cinema with Zoe. By the time I get home, the house is in darkness. Mum and Livi must be fast asleep. I sink down on to the sofa, lost in gloom. The film, about lost love, really got to me. Suddenly I can't stand it any longer. I go on Facebook and lurk on Jem's page. Then I hear a noise outside in the hall and quickly I minimize the site, get to my feet and peer cautiously around the door in the darkness. My sister is tip-toeing upstairs. She freezes in horror when she sees me.

'Don't do that! I thought you were Mum!'

'Where've you been?'

'Shhh!' She glances upstairs apprehensively. 'She'll hear you!'

The penny drops. 'You've been with that loser, Ferret, haven't you?'

She licks her lips nervously then gives me a twisted, little smile. 'So? What if I have?'

'Livi! You are going to get yourself into trouble!'

'What? Like you, you mean?'

I glare at her, torn between the urge to slap her and wanting to sit her down and explain for the umpteenth time why she shouldn't throw herself away on someone like Ferret. She doesn't give me the chance to do either. She disappears upstairs and I wander into the kitchen crossly to make myself a coffee.

I take it upstairs with me to bed and flick through a magazine while I drink it. I must have nodded off because I wake up with a start with the light still on. Then I remember I'd left the computer on Facebook and I nip downstairs to turn it off. I maximize the screen before I switch it off.

Jem has sent me a message.

I miss you, Anna.

What is this, telepathy? One click and I see that he's still online. My heart is racing; my fingers are even faster.

I miss you too.

Back comes the reply and then, before I know it, we are chatting.

> *I didn't steal anything from your father's flat.*
> *No?*
> *You know I didn't. I borrowed some cash, that's all. I was going to put it back.*
> *What about the rest of the stuff?*
> *What, Jude's knickers?*
> *Stop it!*
> *I'm sorry.*
> *What about my dad's watch? And the jewellery?*
> *I didn't take it.*
> *Where is it then?*
> *You're not going to like this.*
> *What?*
> *I think it was an insurance job.*
> *My dad's not a criminal.*
> *Neither am I.*

Leave it there, Anna. It's too painful raking it all up again. But I stare at the screen. *If* Jem is telling the truth and he didn't take those things . . . Well, I didn't take them and Dad didn't take them, that's for sure. So that means there's only one person left to blame for this whole sorry mess.

Jude. She's trying to fiddle the insurance.

The thing is, who do I trust? Jude or Jem?

My fingers type:

I need to see you.

Chapter 39

We arrange to meet at Jem's place the following evening. The next day he rings me in college at lunchtime.

'I finish at six,' he says.

'I'll be round about eight.'

'Can't wait!'

It's so good to hear his voice again that I can't help smiling.

'Who's that?' asks Zoe.

'Nobody special.'

'Yeah right! You've got that same look on your face you used to have when you spoke to Jem. Sort of loopy!'

'Don't be daft!' I say, but she grins and pats me on the knee.

'Good to see you're over Schizo Boy anyway.'

'Jem's not a schizo!' I say automatically, but she's turned away and is chatting to someone else. I take a deep

263

breath and count to ten. When we prove all this has been Jude's fault, she can take that back.

That evening I've just gone upstairs to get ready to meet Jem when Dad appears. He's never away from the place nowadays. I hear him talking to Mum and Livi in the lounge and go back down and pop my head round the door.

'Back again?' I enquire sweetly, but his face is serious.

'I've got something I think you should hear.'

'What is it?' I perch on the edge of the sofa next to Mum. 'Better be quick.'

Dad puts his hands together and stares at the floor, his elbows on his knees. 'There's been a development,' he says and he raises his eyes to mine.

'What sort of development?'

'Five thousand pounds has been stolen from an account.'

I feel my heart plummet.

'Whose account?'

'Jude's.'

Jude's? What's going on here?

'So?'

I stare at him bewildered. Mum places her hand over mine.

'Why has it only just come to light?' she asks.

Dad rubs his brow, then his chin. 'Jude forgot about the account. It's not one she uses very often. We checked all the cards at the time but she forgot about this one. But now her statement has come through and there's five grand missing.'

'Jem wouldn't do that!' cries Livi and I could kiss her. But Dad looks sceptical.

'Look,' I point out reasonably. 'How could he? He'd need a password or a pin number, or something.'

'He must have got hold of them somehow.'

'No way!' Livi explodes.

'It must be Jude,' I explain. 'She must've forgotten she withdrew the money. I do it all the time. I'm for ever thinking I've got more than I have in my account . . .'

'The first withdrawals were made while we were in New York.'

'Oh, come on!' I can feel my temper rising. I don't know what game Jude thinks she's playing here, but she's *not* going to get away with it. 'Jem did not take that money. He couldn't have!'

'Yeah!' Livi agrees. 'You can't pin this one on him!'

'Well, somebody did,' he says flatly and it's obvious he's made up his mind it's Jem.

I lose it. 'Maybe, just maybe, Jude made it up! Have

you thought of that? Maybe your girlfriend is trying to fiddle the insurance!'

'Don't be ridiculous!' snaps Dad. 'She's a lawyer!'

'So?' My voice rises with frustration. 'That doesn't mean she can't commit a crime!' Even to my own ears I sound like an hysterical child.

'Well, we'll find out soon, sure enough. Jude's gone to the police. It's out of my hands.' His tone suggests he's had enough of the whole thing. You can tell he and Jude have had words about it. 'They'll probably want to speak to you at some point, Anna.'

'Right!' I say, getting to my feet. 'Thanks very much! Can I go now?' I stalk out of the house without waiting for an answer.

When I reach the hotel I realize I'm early, but I go round the back to the staff quarters anyway and ring the bell. The door opens immediately but it's not Jem, it's one of his lager-swilling room-mates, the creepy one with the sore red eyes and weak chin who used to drool over the photos of me above Jem's bed. He reminds me of a rat. His eyes light up when he sees me.

'Where's Jem?' I ask.

'Had to go out. He won't be long. Come in and wait for him.'

I brush past him and perch myself gingerly on the end of Jem's bed. There's a stale smell in the room, of unmade beds and unwashed male. No wonder Jem spends as little time here as possible.

'Wanna drink?'

'No thanks.' I can feel him watching me, eyeing me up, and I'm angry with Jem for leaving me alone with him. 'Where's he gone?'

'Got called down to the manager's office.'

'What for?'

'Dunno.' He laughs. 'You never know with Jem. Could be anything.'

I don't bother to reply, then he says, his voice light, teasing, 'Thought you'd been dumped.'

'Did you now?' Not my interpretation of events. I give him a dirty look and get to my feet, my arms wrapped tightly around me, annoyed that Jem would confide in a low-life like him. But then I notice the mass of photos of me has disappeared from the wall and decide that even with his limited number of brain cells, he had probably worked it out for himself.

'Was thinking of asking you out myself,' he says. I feel his piggy little eyes leering at me and dart him a look of disgust. His eyelashes are glued together with blobs of creamy gunge. I feel sick.

To my relief the phone rings and his attention is diverted. Saved by the bell. Literally.

'Manager wants to speak to me too,' he says importantly, putting the phone down. 'Something going on. Won't be long.'

'Take your time.' I breathe a sigh of relief as he goes out. Creep!

I wander listlessly round the room, wishing that Jem would get a move on. I hate it here in this mean, sordid little cell. Above two of the beds – not Jem's, thank goodness – are pictures of glamour models sporting enormous, impossibly circular breasts. I peer in the single wardrobe next to Jem's bed and am surprised how few clothes are in it. I never realized he possessed so little. He always looks cool.

His laptop is on his bed and I notice it's still on. He must've been using it when he was called away. I go to close it down for him and tap the mouse. Loads and loads of folders appear. Some of them have girls' names on them. Megan, Laura, Kally, Holly . . . Maybe I shouldn't be looking at these? Too late now.

I click on to Holly and a photograph appears of a young girl, about Livi's age, smiling provocatively into the camera. Her shoulders are bare. I move on quickly to Laura and see the back view of a young woman walking into a building. It looks like a school. I scroll through the rest of the folder. There are scores of photos of her, none of them posed, as if she's unaware of the photographer's presence. She looks nice. I wonder who she is? She could be Jem's older sister, but he's never mentioned any siblings.

As I close it up I notice a folder with my name on and click on it with a grin. At least he hasn't deleted me completely from his life. I am amazed at the number of photos inside – there must be literally hundreds – some of them posed, most snapshots of me I wasn't even aware he was taking. The mark of a good photographer. He's even got some of me and Livi outside Dad's apartment. I squint at them in surprise.

I don't get this. Something's not right.

Apart from the few days when Dad and Jude were in New York, Jem has never been to their apartment. Let's face it, I haven't either, except for the one overnight stay with Livi. But here's a photo of my sister and me running towards Wharfside, heads down on that very night. Here's another of us by the entrance, shaking raindrops from our hair. It's a good photograph; you can see the raindrops suspended in the air. There's a close-up of Livi, her mouth wide open, laughing, and one of me, pressing the bell.

I didn't know Jem then. Did I?

The penny drops. That was the night I first met him! He was on the bus! Livi was singing out loud and he laughed at her. He must've got off behind us and taken the photographs.

Then the next morning, he was at the bus stop.

And then he was at the shopping centre.

That was no coincidence. He was after me!

Wow! He must have fallen for me that first night on the bus. I knew it! I remember that charge passing between us, like an electric shock. Jem and I were meant to be together.

And stupidly, I'd nearly allowed the evil Jude to split us up. If the police wanted to see me, I'd tell them everything. I'd have to admit we stayed uninvited at Dad's flat and I'm not very proud of that. But at least the truth would come out at last. My father's vile girlfriend had cashed in on the situation and pretended things were missing so she could claim on the insurance. And she'd let poor Jem take the flak for it all! I can't believe how we all fell for it.

All except Livi. She'd never stopped believing in Jem.

It's time for me to put things right. Come on, Jem, hurry up!

I click off my folder and something else catches my eye.

It's another folder with a girl's name on it.

Jude.

He'd been so excited waiting for her to come. Like being on a first date. It was, in a way. He was going to start again, wipe the slate clean.

Well, he wasn't going to confess, obviously. He didn't need to. She'd buy that story of his about the insurance, now he'd planted it in her mind. She'd believe him, he knew she would.

They could go off to London together. Tonight! Leave that sad loser and his stuck-up whore of a girlfriend behind for ever. He didn't know what he'd ever seen in her.

She was one in a million, his Anna. He didn't want to lose her.

Then the manager had called. Wanted to speak to him urgently.

Sod it.

Better be quick.

Chapter 40

'Bastards!'

My head snaps up as the door bangs open and automatically I close the program. My fingers are trembling.

It's Rat-face, I register with relief. But then, as he slams the door behind him angrily, I jump up, terrified he's seen what I'm up to.

'I'm sorry . . .'

'Bloody thieves!'

'What?'

'They took my sodding watch!'

It's not me he's angry with. 'Who did?'

'The pigs, who d'you think?'

'The police?'

He swears again and calls them by a worse name.

'Down there in the manager's office. Said they wanted

me to help them with their inquiries. Nothing to do with me, they said. Then they took my sodding watch!'

He carries on effing and blinding about his watch, his mean little eyes sparking with rage.

'Look,' I say, grabbing my bag. 'I'd better go.'

'Cost me twenty quid, that did!' he yells at me, as if it's all my fault.

'Tell Jem I couldn't wait, yeah?' I say, edging my way towards the door.

A torrent of abuse ensues, mainly concerning what he intends to do to Jem when he gets his hands on him. I stop, my hand on the doorknob.

'Where is he?'

'They've taken him to the police station.'

'What for?' I ask, but I already know the answer.

He shakes his head. 'Dunno. Breaking and entering? Burglary? Something or other. Hope they throw the bloody book at him. Bastard!'

Five minutes earlier I would've been down there defending him. Now, a folder of pictures later, I'm older and wiser. But still, I have one more question for Rat-face.

'Why did they take your watch?'

He eyes me pityingly, like I've got a screw loose or something.

Maybe I have.

'Jem sold it to me. Stolen property, innit?'

I nod. That's all I needed to know.

'No way! No way, man!'

He knew the game was up as soon as he walked into the office and saw the two coppers there waiting for him.

Chapter 41

By the time I get home, Dad has left and Mum and Livi are curled up together watching telly.

'Do the police want to see me?' I ask Mum bleakly.

'Not yet. Tomorrow, I would think.' She grabs my hand. 'You look exhausted.'

'I am.'

'Don't blame yourself for any of this, Anna. You weren't to know what Jem was like.'

I shake her hand away. 'I'm going to bed.'

I stand in the shower under fierce blasts of freezing water, trying to process the implications of what I had seen in that folder marked Jude. By the time I come out I am shaking with cold. It's like I want to punish myself. I choose the roughest, hardest towel I can find and rub my skin till it feels raw, then I crawl into bed and curl up into the foetal position. There's a knock and

Livi's face peers around the door.

'You OK?'

'No,' I say in a low voice.

'Budge up!' She lifts the covers and climbs into bed.
'You're freezing!' she squeals, snuggling down beside me
and hugging me round the waist. There is something
incredibly comforting having my own human hot-water
bottle curled around me. I can feel my heart rate slowing
down, as I match my breath with hers.

'I hate Dad,' she says.

'No you don't.'

'Yes I do!' Her voice is fierce.

'Why?'

'Because he believes the evil Jude, not Jem. So
does Mum.'

I'm silent for a moment. Then I whisper, 'Perhaps
she's not evil.'

'What?'

'Maybe she's telling the truth.'

Livi shoots up to sitting position. 'No way! She said
things were taken from the flat and they weren't. She put
the blame on to Jem. Of course she's evil!'

'Maybe it wasn't like that,' I say, rolling over and
sitting up, my arms around my knees. 'Maybe Jem did
steal those things after all.'

'Anna?' She stares at me aghast. 'I can't believe you said that!'

'How do you know he didn't?'

'Because he said!'

I give a short bitter laugh, like a yelp.

'Jem said lots of things.'

'He *told* me he didn't pinch anything.'

'He was lying.'

'No, he wasn't!'

'He took Dad's watch, Livi. I know he did.'

Her face is livid. 'I don't believe you. You're making it up so that *you* don't get into trouble.'

'What?'

'It was you! You're the thieving scav, not Jem!' She springs out of bed and flings open my wardrobe door, pulling things at random till she finds what she's looking for. 'See!' she says triumphantly, brandishing Jude's top. She flings it on the bed, followed by the incriminating knickers. 'I knew they were there all the time. I wasn't going to say anything till you started blaming it all on Jem.'

I groan. My loyal little sister! 'Don't be daft. You're too flaming nosy for your own good. I only borrowed those. I was going to put them back.'

'Yeah, and Jem told me he was going to put back the

money *he* borrowed. Only he never had time.'

Her pretty, open face is distorted with outrage. Poor Livi. I'd believed that too. Till tonight.

'If he's a thief, so are you!' she persists, her logic irrefutable.

'Look, Livi, there's stuff you don't know about . . .' I say, but she spits back, 'Yeah, well, there's stuff you don't know about too!' and marches out of the bedroom. I sink back against my pillows, thinking when the hell has Jem been filling her head with all this garbage?

But at the moment I've got more pressing questions to worry about. Tonight I viewed hundreds and hundreds of pictures of Jude on Jem's computer. They have totally freaked me out. I've seen:

Jude leaving home, briefcase in hand.

Jude hailing a taxi, getting into a taxi.

Jude entering the office.

Jude leaving the office.

Jude shopping, clutching bags from designer stores.

Jude going into a bar, coming out of a bar.

Jude letting herself into Wharfside.

Jude arm-in-arm with Dad.

Jude talking to me on the street. (I remember that day!)

Jude on her mobile.

Jude with a girlfriend, laughing, carefree.

Jude at a supermarket checkout.

Jude walking through the park.

Jude at a cash-machine.

Jude (long-distance but definitely her) standing at the window of the apartment, looking out over the harbour.

Jude laughing, serious, thoughtful, sad.

Jude with a different hairstyle. A slightly younger version of herself. Where did that one come from . . . ? These two know each other. What the hell is going on?

A crazy, paranoid fear had consumed me. The two of them were in league. It was a set-up. Jude took my dad to New York so Jem could fake a break-in and steal from him! And I was the gullible idiot who made it all possible.

Now, thinking it through logically, I dismiss that idea. More of her stuff was taken than Dad's. Though she might have done that deliberately, for the insurance, like I suspected.

But a wave of common sense washes over me. Come on! For five grand and a few pieces of flash jewellery?

Peanuts to someone earning as much as Jude. She's a successful lawyer, on her way up. Why would she want to risk everything for a few thousand quid? She can earn that in a month.

For Jem?

Jem is a very powerful person. Jem has a way of making you do what he wants. He did it to me.

Zoe was right, he controlled me, like I was his puppet and he was pulling the strings. He cut me off from her. He made me give up on my dreams of a degree in a subject I loved, that I had worked towards all my life. He made me into someone who defaces other people's property, who leaves restaurants without paying, who attacks security guards and runs away, who breaks into her father's apartment and has sex in his bed. And I let him!

He made me fall in love with him. And I thought he loved me too.

I lie there in tears, tormenting myself with images of Jude and him together, laughing at me. Mentally, I scroll through those photographs of Jude again. There were so many of them, loads more than he had ever taken of me. How he must have worshipped her to take all those pictures. And all the time, I was totally devoted to him.

The bastard!

Then, as I peel away the last thin membrane of adoration that has masked my eyes since the day I first met Jem, I see things suddenly in focus so clear and sharp it is painful.

Those pictures. They all had one thing in common.

In every single one of them, Jude was totally oblivious to the fact that her photograph was being taken.

And understanding finally hits me like a two-ton truck.

Jude would never, ever, in a million years have had anything to do with the likes of Jem.

He knew who'd shopped him straight away.

The whore. Discovered at last he'd borrowed her credit card. Well, she obviously didn't need it; it had taken her long enough to find out he'd been milking her account.

Couldn't prove a thing, he'd said, but they'd still arrested him. Laughed in his face, the bastards. Her word against his, and she was the big-shot lawyer.

Yeah, well, they had nothing on him. His Anna would stick up for him. His Anna would get him off.

Chapter 42

The next day, things move rapidly. Dad comes round early, his face grim.

'They need you down at the station for a statement.'

'Have some breakfast first,' says Mum.

I shake my head.

'No, I can't eat a thing. Let's just get it over and done with.'

'I'm coming with you then.' Mum goes out to the hall to grab her coat. 'Livi!' she shouts, 'We've got to go out.'

Livi appears at the top of the stairs in her pyjamas, her hair tousled. 'Where you going?' she asks.

'Police station,' says Dad. 'We're going to nail that little toe-rag once and for all.'

Livi's face turns ugly with fury and she disappears into her bedroom and slams the door.

* * *

Down at the station we are met by a DC Blane who ushers us into an interview room. It's cold and bare, just a desk with chairs either side. He and a woman police officer sit down to question me. I'm scared but I insist my parents leave the room while I talk to them. I don't want them to hear all the details.

They're not unkind, but it's blatantly obvious they think I've been an idiot. I do too. How easy did I make it for Jem?

'Why did you leave him in the apartment on his own?' asks the detective.

'I trusted him.'

His left eyebrow rises, barely perceptible, but enough to convey his opinion. 'Miss Davenport tells us she kept her pin number in her diary. Probably not the best thing to do, in retrospect. Could Jem have had access to this?'

I nod, remembering. 'I saw him reading Jude's diary one day.'

'Good.'

I tell them what they want to know. I don't tell them everything. I don't tell them about us going out graffitiing. We're in enough trouble as it is. I don't tell them about the photos of Jude on the computer either. Why not? I'm a lawyer's daughter. They don't ask and

I don't want to complicate things.

Before long I've given my statement and am reunited with my parents in reception. They put their arms around me and give me a hug.

'What happens now?' I ask.

'They'll charge him and he'll be given a date to appear in court.'

'Will they let him out?'

Dad nods stiffly past me. 'There's your answer.'

Jem is walking out of an interview room accompanied by a man in a suit carrying a briefcase.

'His solicitor?' asks Mum.

'Well, you didn't expect me to represent him, did you?' says Dad wryly. Jem sees me and his face lights up.

'Anna!'

'Come on,' says Dad, taking me firmly by the shoulders. 'Time to go home.' I turn away, my eyes blinded with tears.

In the car on the way home, my phone starts ringing. It's Jem, of course. I ignore the calls, so he texts me. I open it.

Big mistake! I read, then the car swerves as my phone is snatched out of my hand.

'What are you doing?' I shout.

'I'll take care of that!' says Dad grimly. He switches the

phone off and sticks it in his pocket. I stare out of the window, furious.

At home the house is quiet. Livi has left for school. I go upstairs and get my things together. When I come back down, Mum and Dad, who are in cohorts in the kitchen, turn to look at me.

'Where are you going?' asks Dad.

'College, where do you think?'

'I'll give you a lift.'

'There's no need.'

'No bother.'

I know what he's doing. Making sure I go nowhere near Jem. 'Can I have my phone?' I ask.

'No. I want to hang on to it for a while.'

I roll my eyes. 'Why?'

'For your own protection. I don't want you to have anything to do with that man.'

'Neither do I! Don't you trust me?'

'Yes! Of course we do!' says Mum.

'*He* doesn't!' I scowl at Dad.

'I do,' he says, but I don't believe him. Then he adds, his voice gentle. 'It's him I don't trust, Anna, not you. I don't want him talking to you. I'll keep it for a day or two, that's all. He'll soon give up if he can't get through.'

Yeah? You don't know him like I do. I blink hard, trying not to fall apart. Don't be nice to me, Dad, please. If you're cross with me I can cope, but if you're nice I'll dissolve into a wailing, blubbery mess.

'Keep it. What difference does it make?'

I get through the day somehow. Dad insists on picking me up, which is a pain because I'm free last lesson but I'd forgotten to tell him, so I have to hang around.

I go into the library to wait for him. It's busy in there, all the computers and most of the tables full. I sit down and work for a while but my brain soon gives up. I'm knackered.

I can see Zoe seemingly working away at a computer. But when I go up to speak to her, I see she's on Facebook.

'Skiver!' I say and she jumps. We're not supposed to go on social sites at college but we all do.

'I've finished now,' she says.

'Can I check mine?'

She gets up obligingly and I log into my account.

Jem has posted a comment on my wall.

Anna Williams is a thieving, lying slag.

Underneath Livi has posted one too.

Yeah, you're right.

I gasp. Which one hurts the most?

Quickly I log on to my messages. There are loads from Jem. I scroll through them. I wish I hadn't.

The stuff that is written there is vile. They all follow the same theme. I'd led him along. *I'd* stolen the money, the jewellery, not him. Then I'd left him to carry the can. He'd loved me but I'd let him down and now I wouldn't even answer my phone. I was this, I was that – horrible, abusive labels that make me moan in pain, like I've been punched in the stomach.

Hearing me, Zoe comes up and reads over my shoulder, inhaling in horror.

'Psycho!' she growls. 'You don't have to read that rubbish!' She leans forward and deletes them all, one after the other. Then she leads me to a table and sits me down. I'm shaking.

'What brought this on?' she asks.

'I shopped him to the cops.'

'Good for you! Now you can forget all about him. He's out of your life, for ever.'

She talks me through it, calming me down. Jem has done his worst, she explains. What more could he do? It's over.

And I almost believe her, there in the sane, industrious world of the busy library.

Till I get outside.

It was easy. Throw it up, one colour, bright red.

Nobody noticed him at the college, just another student.

Straight up the drainpipe on to the roof, dress up the wall in seconds, slide back down again.

Job done.

On to the next one.

Chapter 43

I don't notice it at first. When the bell goes and I walk out of college with Zoe, I pause on the top step to look for Dad. I know he'll be here somewhere, waiting for me.

I spot him straight away. He's got out of the car and is staring up at the college building. He's not the only one. As students pour out through the doors and mill about in the car park, waiting for buses, chatting among themselves, getting into cars, I notice something catching their eye above my head. People start pointing. A crowd gathers, looking up at the building. Most of them look stunned; one or two are sniggering.

'What's going on?' asks Zoe and she bounds down the steps and looks back. 'Oh, no!' she breathes, her eyes widening with horror. 'Don't look, Anna.'

I take the steps two at a time and turn around to gaze up at the building. Just below the flat roof of the main reception, a message has been sprayed in huge scarlet letters.

Anna Williams is a Bitch and a Slut!

Bizarrely, my first thought is: That's not up to your usual standard, Jem. You must have thrown that one up quickly, up there on the roof in the middle of the day. Did you hang upside down to do it? I've seen you do that before. Shame you had to sacrifice aesthetics for speed.

Still, he'd managed to sign it. Only now the savage head of JAWS has disappeared. His tag is back to the solitary, but just as vicious, Fin.

Good. Now leave me alone.

I feel oddly disconnected from it all, like I'm an observer, not the subject, of all this vitriol. I can hear people whispering. Mates gather round, outraged, giving me support, and weirdly, it's me that's consoling them. 'It's OK,' I say to Ben, who is shocked to the core. 'Don't worry, I'm fine.' My dad comes towards me and puts out his arms and I turn into him, my face pressed against his chest. His arms lock around me and I can feel him trembling. Poor Dad. I pat his back, comforting him.

I hate Jem for what he's done to me. Even more, I hate him for what he's putting Dad through. No father should see his daughter's name blackened like this.

What did Dad ever do to him?

We drive home together, silent, chastened. As we draw up outside the house, we stare in horror at the front door.

He's been here too.

Chapter 44

This time he's written:

Bitches! Whores! The lot of you!

Dad manages to get rid of it by the time Mum gets home from work. It's not easy. He tries detergent first, then white spirit from the shed. In the end he jumps in the car and comes back with some paintstripper.

When Mum arrives to find the paint stripped from her front door, we usher her straight inside. Dad is really sweet with her. He makes her a cup of tea and sits her down and tells her what's happened. I've read that people go white with shock and I never thought it was true, but Mum's face drains completely of colour when she hears what he's written. Dad plays it down.

'Don't worry. It's just stupid, spiteful insults. He can't do anyone any harm.'

He's right. To be honest, I'm not scared of Jem. I just feel numb. But I'm so glad my father is here to take charge and I know Mum is too.

And then, as if on cue, his phone rings and it's Jude on the line, wanting to know where he is.

'I'm at home,' he says, adding quickly. 'At Maggie's.'

Mum and I can't help exchanging a wry look. Bit of a Freudian slip that. Dad's been spending so much time here over the last few weeks, since all this trouble broke, he's starting to think of it as home again.

'It's a bit awkward at the moment . . .' he says and though we're hearing only one side of the conversation it's obvious she wants him back at the flat. I can hear her voice, high and agitated, though it's hard to make out what she is saying, and I feel a familiar spasm of irritation.

'Calm down,' says Dad. 'Take a deep breath.' But she keeps on talking and his expression changes. 'Are you sure it's him?' he says. Then, 'Have you told the police?' When he closes his phone his face is fraught with tension.

'What's happened?'

'Now Jem has been charged, Jude decided to look at the CCTV images after all.' He licks his lips nervously.

'So?'

'She recognizes him.'

I stare at him blankly. So they *did* know each other. I was right after all. 'How come?'

'Jude was his defence lawyer. She got him off some charge a year or two ago on a technicality, some petty crime or other. Privately she thought he was lucky to get away with it.'

'I don't get it . . .'

'His name is Jermaine Smith. It was at her last practice. He's one of hundreds of young thugs who have passed through her hands. After she got him off, Jermaine made a nuisance of himself. Started ringing her up, demanding to see her. Seemed to think there was some sort of special bond between them because she'd defended him successfully in court. Didn't seem to understand she was only doing her job.' He shrugs. 'It happens. Half the people we represent are unhinged in some way. When she moved down here, it stopped.'

I think back to the time Jem told me about his car-crash of a life. The list of women who had let him down. The most recent was a woman who'd left him for some old guy with more money.

That was Jude. And the 'old guy' she'd left him for was Dad.

At least, that's how he'd perceived it in his twisted mind. He'd thought he had some sort of romantic *thing* going with her. That she'd got him off because there was something going on between them.

I sit there stunned, trying to take it all in.

It's sick. What is wrong with him? Couldn't he see she was just doing her job? She was a lawyer, that's all, a professional, albeit a very attractive one, who had defended him successfully before she moved on to her next brief. End of story.

But not for Jem.

Jem is the one who's got to be in control. Why didn't I listen to you, Zoe? He'd created that entire relationship in his head. Hence the photographs. As far as he was concerned, they loved each other and it was my wicked father who was coming between them.

Poor, deluded Jem.

And then the truth smacks me in the face.

None of this was about me! The only reason he went out with me was to get at Jude! Jem had used me and I'd allowed him to.

I taste the bitter bile of resentment rising in my throat. This is all her fault!

Why didn't she warn me? Why didn't she tell me what a weirdo I was going out with? Why did she let me get involved with him in the first place?

But even as I ask the questions, the answer's obvious.

308

Because she didn't know.

James was my boyfriend, I'd boasted to her. Nice, pleasant, well-bred James who was at Oxford, studying Medicine. Pretty common name really. She'd invited us round for dinner, couldn't wait to meet him, but I'd ignored the invitation. I had to. I was lying through my teeth just to impress her.

It wasn't Jude's fault. It was mine.

'This guy is unpredictable,' says Dad, getting to his feet. 'I'm going back to the apartment. Jude's there on her own.'

'You don't think he'd do anything, do you?' asks Mum, her eyes round with fear.

'He's got photographs of her.' My voice is a whisper, but Mum and Dad stare at me as if I'd shouted it out loud.

'On his computer.'

Dad looks stricken.

'Go!' says Mum.

'He won't hurt her!' I protest but my words sound hollow, even to me. I try to explain. 'He's just got this thing about women, that's all . . . He thinks we all let him down.'

Dad makes for the door. 'That,' he says, 'is exactly what worries me.'

He wasn't going to stop there. No way. Anna had it coming to her, the bitch. How could she do this to him? He'd thought she was different, but they were all the same when it came down to it. Bitches! Whores!

That's what he'd sprayed on the front door. He felt like spraying it over the whole town.

And then the door had opened and Livi had come out.

Little Livi.

Chapter 45

After Dad leaves, Mum says she'd better make us something to eat.

'I'm not hungry,' I say, but she ignores me and starts bunging pieces of chicken in the microwave and peeling veg. I think she needs to keep busy.

'Where was Livi going after school?' she asks.

'I don't know. She'd left before we came back from the police station.' I'm exhausted. This horrible day seems to be going on and on and all I want to do is go to bed.

'Well, give her a ring and tell her dinner will be ready soon.'

'Dad's got my phone!' I remind her.

'Use the house one.'

I do as I'm told but her number goes straight to answer phone. 'Her mobile's switched off.'

Mum tuts. 'Ring her friends then.'

'Who?'

'I don't know! You know who she goes round with more than I do!'

Actually, I haven't got a clue who Livi is keeping company with nowadays. She changes her friends as often as she changes her clothes and, personally, I've been too absorbed in what's been going on in my own life lately to notice! I ring round a few girls from her class whose numbers I find in the telephone directory. No one has seen her. I distinctly get the impression that Livi doesn't go round with them any more.

'No luck?' says Mum. 'Keep trying.'

I roll my eyes. What's the big deal? Livi can eat when she comes in.

'Try Cora Pugh,' suggests the next girl I ring.

'Cora Pugh? Wasn't that the kid Livi had a fight with? No way!' I shake my head in disbelief.

'Ring her,' says Mum. I flick through the directory until I find a Pugh who lives on the estate near school and ring them. It's the right number. Cora comes on the line.

'Do you know where Livi is?' I ask.

'Livi who?'

'Williams?' I say sweetly. How many Livis are there?

'Who wants to know?'

'Her sister.'

'What for?' she asks rudely.

I suppress the urge to tell her to mind her own business. I can't say, 'Her tea's ready,' or she'd laugh out loud at me. So instead I say, 'My mother's concerned that she hasn't come home from school yet.' And as soon as I say it, I realize that's exactly why Mum has asked me to ring around.

There's silence, then she says suspiciously, 'What's this got to do with me?'

'Nothing. I just thought you might know where she is because you're a friend of hers.'

'Yeah, I am. She's my bezzie mate.' She sounds flattered. For the life of me, I can't imagine Livi feeling the same way about her.

'D'you know where she is then?' I persist.

'Dunno. She left school at lunchtime.'

'Lunchtime!'

'Nowt to do with me!' she says immediately.

'No, I know that! Only, do you know why?'

There's a pause.

'Maybe she was going to meet someone.'

'Who?'

'Dunno. That's all I know. Got to go.'

She's on her guard now, it's obvious. I'm not going to get another word from her.

I don't need any more information anyway. I've had my suspicions for a while. It's pretty obvious who she's skiving off school to spend time with.

Ferret.

Also known as Steven Ferris, to give him his proper title.

I put the phone down and gaze sorrowfully at my poor mum. What on earth did she do to deserve daughters like us?

He'd thought she might run back inside when she saw what he'd written but she didn't.

She just stood there and read it then turned round, cool as a cucumber, and said, 'No we're not. Not all of us.'

Chapter 46

'Where the hell has she got to?' says Mum when I tell her Livi left school at lunchtime. She looks in such a state, I admit that I think she's with Ferret.

'Tell her to get home, NOW!' she says, through gritted teeth, and I want to oblige, I really do, but the trouble is, I haven't a clue where Ferret hangs out and the only Ferrises in the phone book deny all knowledge of him. I try Cora again but she doesn't answer. I try Livi but it clicks straight through. And all the time my poor mum is pacing the floor and biting her nails down to her elbows, and the hands of the clock are moving on, and there is no sign of my little sister.

'I'm phoning your father!' she says at last.

When Dad comes back again, this time he's got Jude in tow. Both of them look shaken.

'What's up?' I ask as he shoulders his way

through the door.

'You don't want to know,' he mutters.

'Yes I do,' says Mum. 'What's happened now?'

Dad looks at Jude. 'It's all over the front wall of Williams & Barnes,' she says, her voice trembling.

'What is?' Mum looks from one to the other. 'Tell me!'

'Filth,' says Dad bitterly. 'Stinking, foul abuse about Jude and me. We've just had a phone call from security.'

My heart sinks. It's Jem, getting his own back.

'Have you found Livi?' asks Dad.

Mum shakes her head. 'We've tried everywhere. I don't know where she is. Anna thinks she might be with this boy she used to know called Fer . . . Steven Ferris – but I'm not sure . . .'

Her voice trails away and she stares at him miserably. It's like they understand each other without having to speak.

'I'm calling the police!' he says decisively and takes out his phone.

'Why?' I say in surprise. 'She'll turn up, she always does. She's done this before.'

Everyone looks at me sadly. Then Jude moves over to Mum and places her arm round her shoulders.

'Do it,' she says to Dad. 'Do it now.'

He could see straight away, Livi wasn't scared of him.

She was on his side.

Livi wasn't scared of anything.

He should've picked her in the first place, he thought. He'd made the wrong choice. He'd selected the wrong sister.

Livi understood. She knew it was all Jude's fault.

Livi would do anything for him.

Anything.

Chapter 47

I must be the dimmest person in the world. It had simply never occurred to me that Livi was with Jem.

Even when the squad car arrives, I still don't get how serious the situation is. They've already checked out Ferret and confirmed that he hasn't seen Livi for days. Apart from being an annoying little shit, he seems to be harmless.

'We've got an alert out for Jermaine Smith,' says the officer. It's DC Blane, the one I spoke to at the station.

'He's got her,' says Jude. 'I know he has!'

Mum nods in agreement, trying not to cry.

I stare at them blankly. It's obvious when you think about it, she's with him. They all look terrified.

'Don't worry.' I say. 'He hasn't kidnapped her, if that's what you're worried about.'

'You don't know that,' says Dad.

'She's run off with him!' I say. 'She's mad about him.' The world and his wife could be against Jem but Livi would be there for him through thick and thin.

'I think she's right,' whispers Mum.

'Nevertheless, we'll put a Missing Persons out on her straight away.'

Blane walks outside to speak privately into his radio and Mum and Dad exchange anxious looks, afraid to speak.

'What's your concern?' asks Dad when he returns.

The detective hesitates, like he's not sure how much information he should be divulging.

'Jermaine Smith has history.'

'What sort of history?'

'I'm afraid I'm not at liberty to say, sir.'

'I represented him last year,' Jude's voice rings out crisply. 'He had petty larceny on his record, that's all.'

'Really?' says DC Blane, raising his eyebrows, and we know there's more to it than that. 'Then you're obviously not aware that Smith has an obsessive, addictive personality. When he meets someone he likes he falls madly in love with them. Literally. He won't take no for an answer.'

Jude flushes, like she's been caught out not doing her job properly. 'Now,' he says, 'if I could just take a few details.'

We give him all the information we can about Livi and he scribbles it down. Meanwhile my parents become visibly more distressed.

After a while my father says savagely, 'If he harms one hair of her head . . . !' and I say, 'He wouldn't do that, Dad!' but my words are cut off as the officer's radio crackles into life.

'What are you defending him for?' says my father through gritted teeth as Blane goes back outside to answer it.

'I'm not! I just know he wouldn't hurt Livi. He wouldn't hurt anyone. Not in that way.'

'You don't know the first thing about him!' says Dad furiously.

He's right. Let's face it, Jem has always been a complete mystery to me. That was part of his charm. But I am absolutely convinced, whatever else he has done, Jem would never deliberately harm my kid sister.

Then DC Blane returns to the room and clears his throat.

'I'm afraid,' he says, 'there's been an incident.'

When he told her where he was going next she'd said she'd come with him.

He'd actually hesitated. 'It's dangerous,' he'd warned her, but she'd laughed. She was really up for it.

You could hardly blame her. Jude had messed up her life, just like she'd messed up his.

Chapter 48

We tear through town, blue lights flashing, siren wailing. Bizarrely, all I can think is, Livi would love this.

But Livi's not here.

As we approach Dad's apartment we can see the flashing lights of police cars up ahead. They've closed the road. The area below the building has been taped off and floodlights are directed up towards the flat roof of the warehouse. It looks as if they've evacuated the whole building, because a small crowd has gathered across by the harbour.

We get out of the car and run towards Wharfside. As I peer up at the roof I can make out a small figure looking down at us.

'It's Livi!'

There's a small flash of light. I wonder what it is until a second figure appears beside her. It's Jem with his camera.

A guy holding a megaphone who seems to be in charge comes over to greet us.

'My name's Phil,' he introduces himself, and starts explaining to Mum and Dad what's going on. I look back up at the roof at the two figures silhouetted against a background of stars. Suddenly Jem's favourite song floods into my mind and I'm drowning in terror.

And when no hope was left in sight
On that starry, starry night.
You took your life
As lovers often do . . .

Jem raises his hand and waves. He can see me. I wave back at him. I don't know what else to do.

A van appears and police in flak jackets spill out of it. Phil mentions a 'hostage situation'. I stare at the guys in horror. This is crazy; they look like a riot squad. For all I know, these guys have got guns.

'He's not armed!' I interrupt.

'Can you be sure of that?' Phil turns to me. I shake my head in disbelief.

'He hasn't taken her against her will!' I explain, but no one's listening.

'Oh my God!' Dad points up to the roof.

Jem is leaning over the edge, his head and upper body

dangling in mid-air. The crowd gasps.

'Where's Livi?' screams Mum. My sister has disappeared from sight. 'Livi!'

'It's OK! Shhh!' I grab Mum's arm to calm her down. 'He's tagging, that's all.'

'What?' Mum clings to me in terror.

'He's doing graffiti. She'll be hanging on to his legs. She's fine.'

Mum sobs. 'How do you know that?'

'I've done it myself.'

We watch with our hearts in our mouths, as, upside down, Jem sprays an F on the warehouse wall. Then he wriggles his way back up to the roof, moves along a bit, and does the same manoeuvre again, only this time it's a U.

The tension lifts and a ripple of amusement passes through the crowd as it becomes obvious what he's writing. When he's finished, the crowd bursts into applause and Jem stands up and takes a bow. Livi appears beside him and he raises her hand in triumph.

It's OK. He's loving this. So is she. There's nothing sinister going on. He's just being a bad boy.

'He's a graffiti artist,' I explain, weak with relief. 'He was pissed off. That's all. Now he's got it out of his system.'

'As far as we're concerned, he's dangerous,' says Phil curtly and walks away to confer with the heavy squad.

Jem plays to the crowd and they egg him on, enjoying the free entertainment. Better than telly, this.

Using the megaphone, Phil tries to talk him down. He responds by dangling upside down again and spraying his opinion of him and the police in general on the front of the building. The crowd love it.

I gulp. Watching Jem's antics from this angle, with a crick in my neck, unable to take my eyes away from the drama unfolding on the roof above me, I can see clearly what a dangerous game he is playing. One slip and he'd be dead. That's the thrill of it. He's having a ball, up there, taunting the police, sticking a finger up to them.

Be careful, Jem. Don't fall. I know you're the maestro, I know you're as agile and sure-footed as a cat, but even cats have only nine lives.

Then, to my surprise, he adds his signature, Fin, for all the world to see. Finally, he's come out. He's revealed his identity. Why would he do that?

My blood chills as I recall the words of Jem's poem, the one he dedicated to me.

I would go down for loving you
But if I did, I'd bring you too.

And if you sent me down to hell
I'd take you there with me as well.

But that was meant for me, not Livi!

High up on the rooftop, my sister is having a wonderful time. She's never had such a spellbound audience before in her life. The excitement is getting to her; she's leaping about now with a spray can in her hand.

She wants a go.

Instantly, cold with fear, I snatch the megaphone from Phil's hand.

'NO! DON'T LET HER, JEM!'

I shouldn't have interfered. No one tells Jem Smith what to do. Though I think, for a moment, he hesitates.

But it's too late. Livi is already down on her stomach and has disappeared from sight and automatically he drops to his knees to hold her legs. Her head appears above the parapet, commando style. She waves the paint can at us, milking her audience, and the crowd cheers.

Beside me Dad yells, 'GET BACK, LIVI! GET BACK!' But this is her moment and nothing is going to spoil it. Mum presses her face into his chest, afraid to look, as Livi leans over the edge of the building and hangs upside down.

I watch, afraid to breathe, as, concentrating hard, she

laboriously executes a perfect-shaped heart, the right way up, with the spray can. I know, I just know, her tongue will be sticking out between her white teeth with concentration, just like it did when she was a little kid. The crowd is silent. Heads back, everyone bar Mum watches her like a hawk as, inside the heart, she painstakingly writes

Sweet Livi. Her only fault ever was to love people too much.

He'd seen Anna down there and without thinking he'd waved.
His heart had flipped over when she'd waved back.

She still loved him. She understood. Of course she did.

No one could prevent them from loving each other, no one could tear them apart. They'd had their best moments on rooftops, like this. They were king.

He wanted to call down to her then, to tell her this, to tell her it was going to be all right.

But the next minute a van had pulled up and the riot squad spilt out.

It was too late.

That's when he got down to business.

Chapter 49

It all happens in a flash.

Livi finishes off with a flourish and throws her arms out in triumph, as graceful as a trapeze artist. The crowd whoops and applauds.

You show-off! is my immediate sour thought. You're loving every minute of this.

She dangles upside down for a few seconds, savouring her moment of glory.

At this point I'm actually jealous. *I'm* the graffiti artist, not her; I'm the one who's been out tagging with Jem night after night! I've been up on that very roof with him myself, only minus the audience.

But I never had the nerve to go over the edge like she did. So Livi hogs the limelight, as usual, and even though I know she's going to get hell for this, part of me wishes it was me up there.

I say something to my mother like, 'It's OK, Mum, you can look now.' Mum peers upwards, terrified, her knuckles pressed against her mouth.

Above us, Livi twists and jerks, like she's trying to heave herself back upwards but doesn't quite know how. She stops and hangs there for a moment, out of breath, like a crumpled balloon, and I start to feel uneasy. The crowd waits, all attention again.

It's obvious it's going to be harder to get back up than she thought it would be. *If* she thought at all. She's tired now.

I can feel cold fingers of fear clutching at my throat. Beside me, Mum is stiff with tension.

'Careful, Livi,' I whisper.

She flops about a bit and I can sense her panic, even from down here. I can hear Jem's voice shouting instructions and suddenly she does one massive, desperate, convulsive movement, and arches her body upwards. Jem's head and shoulders appear, his hand reaching out to grab her, and at the same time there is an almighty explosion of noise and police burst on to the roof behind them.

And I don't know what happens next.

Maybe he missed her altogether.

Maybe the noise made him jump and he let go.

338

Maybe he couldn't hang on any more and she just slipped from his grasp.

But she's hurtling towards us and she lands on the road. It's all over in a second.

As simple as that.

End of story.

She wanted to . . .
I never meant . . .
It wasn't me . . .
She wanted to!

Chapter 50

Where are you, Livi?

My beautiful, blonde, bursting-with-life baby sister?

Where have you gone?

It's so quiet here without you. Quiet as the grave.

I can't bear it.

Though for weeks it was manic. Your smiling face was on the telly, you see. And the front page of the paper.

So many flowers left at Wharfside. The traffic couldn't get through. You had no idea how popular you were.

So many cards. Hundreds of them. From family, friends, neighbours, teachers, dinner ladies, shopkeepers . . . People I never even knew you knew. Little kids you stopped and spoke to; old people you said hello to . . . They all loved you.

Shame they waited till you were gone to say how amazing you are.

Were.

I can't believe you're dead.

Your friends set up a Facebook page for you. They've called it: *Livi: the brightest star*. You lit up the lives of so many people, you see. I wish you could see what they've written. I spend hours on it, reading the comments.

Zoe wrote: *I miss your smile*.

I do too.

Ben wrote: *I loved the laughs we had together*.

I never thought about you when I dumped him. Sorry, Livi.

Ferret wrote: *You were the best*.

Bit late for that.

Some of your teachers have joined your page and said what a lovely student you were.

Who'd have thought you had so many fans? Seems like you were everyone's best friend.

Even Cora's. She wrote how she will never take off the bracelet you gave her. She added a picture of herself wearing it.

That was my bracelet, Livi. I wondered where it had gone.

It's OK, I don't mind. She can keep it.

Everyone's posting pictures.

Most are recent, of you with your cropped hair and your cool clothes, arms flung round someone's shoulders, beaming or pouting into the camera.

Some are years old, when your hair was long, your knees were scuffed and your smile had a gap in it.

I'd forgotten how sweet you were.

I thought you would live for ever. Now all I'm left with is a page on a website and a folder full of cards and newspaper articles.

I miss you, Livi.

One day someone posted a picture of you that took my breath away. You were laughing out loud in it, your blonde head tilted back, your mouth open wide, displaying your perfect white teeth. Even with your eyes practically closed, your face sparkled with life and energy and mischief. You were glowing.

It was you, completely you, in a way the hundreds of other posed pictures failed to be.

And I knew. Even before I saw his name, I knew who had posted it.

His parting gift to me.

It was the last one he ever took of you. Up on the roof. You were having the very best time of your life.

Minutes later, you were dead.

Jem caused chaos wherever he went. But he never

meant that to happen, Liv, not for a minute. I'm convinced of it.

It's my fault. All of it. For falling in love with him. And you're the only one who could understand, because you did too.

In the confusion Jem got away. I stared at you lying there like a broken doll and I couldn't take it in.

I still can't.

I looked up and saw him gazing down at you. Then he leapt into space and landed on the roof of the next building, one storey down.

I don't know what he did after that, but I can guess.

He would have kept going forwards, scaling walls, jumping obstacles, dropping into hiding places. He'd have dived, vaulted, spun, flipped, climbed, straddled, rotated and pushed his way to freedom.

Jem just kept on running, without a backward glance, till he was gone.

He left me.

And you left me too.

Where are you, Livi?

Please answer me.